AN CONWAY
COLD BORDER

1

First published in Great Britain by Wallbank Books 2024 Copyright © Andy Conway 2024

The right of Andy Conway to be identified as the authors of this work has been asserted by him in accordance with the Copyright, Designs and patent Act,

1988

ISBN: 9798321492178

Cover design by Simon Moody at Wallbank Art

To

Jack Turner

1

SEPTEMBER 13TH, 2001. OXFORD.

Two days after the big event, he'd never seen so many people buying newspapers: extra piles of them on the stands, people poring over them as they walked. The televisions crowding the electronics shop window showed the same loop of images that were now sickeningly familiar, even though they less than 48 hours old.

A hazy, pixelated shot of two towers, shimmering in heat. The outline of a ghost bird smashing in behind. A plume of flame spurting out. Businesswomen cowering in a gutter. The North Tower collapsing in smoke. A cloud chasing people down a street. A fireman looming through fog. They ran on a loop on every TV in the world, new images added every hour as the story thickened, and now most were of that great pile of smoking rubble.

A scene out of Dante's Inferno: Ninth Bolgia. Pandemonium. Ground Zero.

Crowds gathering in the square before the two-centuries-old fake Jacobethan Oxford Council House. Office workers stopped, coffee cups in hand, a few with little paper Stars and Stripes flags. The Union flag above the council house hung at half-mast. The mayor and several council officials filed out down steps to the square, to lead a minute's silence. All over the UK this scene would be repeated, as in every city, town and village, people gathered to do something, show solidarity, find some outlet for their helplessness.

Curtis ignored them, walking on past.

Three hundred yards from Carfax Tower, he found the Spirenet cyber cafe and entered, enjoying the waft of cool air, relief from the late summer heat outside. Banks of monitors showed the same images as the televisions, some frozen, a few moving. There was only one story in the world.

But there was about to be another.

Keeping his head down, the baseball cap hiding his face from the CCTV cameras he'd scoped before, he walked to the reception desk. He booked a computer for an hour with his false ID, signed a fake signature and sat before a monitor, his back to the wall.

He took a floppy disk from his leather document folder and inserted it. The computer sucked it in. An Explorer folder opened and displayed the contents of the floppy. A single file titled *poem.txt*.

He double-clicked it and a text file shot open. He stabbed Alt+A, switched his index finger to C and then in a Netscape browser window logged into his alt/conspiracy account.

He pasted the poem into a new message. It rolled off the screen. A long post. Perhaps too long. They said people weren't prepared to read long posts on the internet — that was what books were for — attention spans were shortening. But this wasn't the case in those dark corners of the net where conspiracy theories bloomed. Long posts were good. The more detail the better. But on this site, no one had posted a poem before. It would become immediately clear to anyone reading the post that this was a confession from the depths of the dirty war on terror that was in the process of being launched — and that it was so much more.

He reckoned it would be up no more than 24 hours before it was taken down. The site would crash. For perhaps half a day. And when it was back up, his post would be gone. That was the usual method of censoring the net. But his poem would be copied and distributed and never quite stamped out, like persistent knotweed.

A deep breath.

This was the moment the world would change, and it was not the scenes on every TV and computer screen and newspaper. It was this.

No one would see what he'd done. Not for years. Ten, maybe even twenty years. But this was the beginning of the new world. And when it came, someone would remember this and go back and see that he had told them and it had all come to bear.

He was announcing the future world order. The end of it all.

The world would come crashing down around them and make those twin towers look like a pair of kids' fireworks.

He pressed Post, closed his chat window, ejected his floppy disk and, keeping his baseball cap low over his face, walked back out to the street.

In five minutes he was back at his desk in the Ministry of Defence.

2

THE NIGHT SKY BULLETED with stars was all John Blackwood could see. Lapping water at his dinghy, lurching, rocking. He was all out to sea. His ribs burning like he was pierced by a spear. He was thinking of the lance that pierced Jesus on the cross and wondering if that was the blow that killed him. A mouthful of vinegar on a sponge. His legs broken. Scarred and bloody and at the end of it all.

The start of it all.

He wasn't Christian so it made no sense that he would think that. Was he converting at the moment of his death? There was no priest to give the last rites. Not here in a Combat Rubber Raiding Craft out to sea.

Livid stars in black sky. Nightfruit.

And then there were voices calling out over the waves. Voices in a language he couldn't understand.

"He looks dead."

"Get him. We can use him."

"Get a boat hook."

"There. The rope!"

Yes, that was it. He'd crawled into the dinghy on the beach.

The beach of death.

Where it had all ended.

Where it had all begun.

He'd watched his daughter walk off with the money. He'd killed Brand on that beach. A burning farmhouse and a hundred corpses. A Zodiac dinghy on the beach, and a boat of some kind waiting out there in the dark sea.

The dinghy tugged, sliding suddenly, being pulled.

He lolled over to one side, in the recovery position. Another lurch and he rolled onto his back again.

Someone was standing over him. Dark figure. Peacoat, beanie, Arran sweater.

Hands reached for him.

Searing pain ricocheted through him.

He might have screamed.

A clank of metal reverberated as he was dragged up, and in the moment before blackness swallowed him, he realized it wasn't a fishing boat that had been waiting out there at sea at all.

It was a submarine.

3

JASKE SENSED THE SUBMARINE had surfaced again: the pressure in her ears of the rising and the sudden keel as they broke water. The hull clanged and resonated. Jaske listened carefully to the sounds of activity that echoed down the alleyway.

The girls huddled together, locked in their bunk room, dreading what would come next.

"That's the cargo," Jaske said. "They're unloading it."

"I thought *we* were the cargo," Mimmi spat.

"No, we'll be rescued," Frida said, quite simply. She had said it a thousand times, so that the words meant nothing now.

Jaske turned and looked at their faces: ten scared girls who looked to her for leadership, for hope, when she had none to give. She might have been the most senior but she didn't feel it. She was only eight years older than them.

Fresh out of Sámi university. A research assistant. Her first job. Just starting out her life. But already old in their eyes: these girls who had only left home for the first time to start university.

How quickly the bravado and the cynical air of cool had evaporated when confronted by real peril. It would with anyone. They were in the hands of criminals.

She had to get them out of this somehow. Get them home.

It was her duty of care.

But there was no hope. She was powerless.

"The pallet they loaded," Jaske insisted. "I saw them load it at Hidra. A pallet of sello-wrapped packages. Heroin, probably. That's the cargo."

Something clanged along the side of the sub.

"And that's a boat," said Jaske.

"A police boat," Frida cried. "We're being rescued."

Jaske shook her head, though she hated to quash Frida's childish hope. It was clear from the shouts and calls of the men that this was all business. "It will be the boat that is taking the cache ashore."

"And what shore would that be?" Mimmie demanded.

"I don't know," Jaske said. "I'm not party to their plans."

"Scotland," said Helve. "We sailed underwater for an hour or more. It has to be Scotland."

"Maybe one of the Hebridean islands," Sophie said.

Scotland sounded right, Jaske thought. "They're smuggling drugs into Britain perhaps. Maybe that's what this is all about."

"And women," said Olivia. "Us."

Several of the girls cried out like wailing mourners.

"Wherever it is, we're far away from home."

"We're going to be sold."

"I want to go home. I want my mother."

Jaske swallowed a ball of rage and counted to ten under her breath. It wasn't their fault. They were women but had regressed into little girls since this had all begun. Little girls who cried for their mothers. They sniffled and sobbed and clung to each other. Of course they did. Anyone would.

"It's all right," Jaske said. "Don't be scared."

But she knew it wasn't all right.

"Listen," she said.

Everyone held their breath, except Olivia, still keening like a cat in the cold.

"It's quiet. They've gone ashore."

"They're taking the drugs," Mimmi said. "We'll be next."

Jaske said nothing but knew Mimmi was probably right.

The silence descended on them and there was nothing to do but sit and wait. They sat in silence for an hour or more, some of the girls getting ready to disembark, before the shouting began again.

And this time it was not all business.

She caught snatches of Norwegian and Russian from the men, panic in their voices. Whatever their plan was — and she knew it involved drugs and money and selling off girls, and she knew it was so big that they could buy a fucking submarine — it had failed.

"Something has gone badly wrong," Jaske said.

"That's good," said Frida. "We're being rescued."

Shouts echoed down the gangway. A fierce argument. A debate about what to do. More fuss, and then a boat — maybe two boats — thumped alongside.

"There's a stranger on board," Jaske hissed. "They're arguing about him. Whether to let him live or die."

"Maybe it's us they're arguing about," said Mimmi. "Whether we live or die."

Someone screamed, "What about the money?"

They all heard it. Jaske shushed the girls, franticly whispering about what this could mean.

Again, more than one of the crew screamed this question. *What about the money?*

"It seems that the money is gone," Jaske said. "And the drugs."

"Perhaps a police bust has foiled the whole operation," Frida cried.

"The only thing that isn't gone is us," Mimmi said.

Everyone cried as the sub descended again with a sudden lurch.

More arguing, fists banging on the iron walls. They talked in Norwegian about gunshots, explosions, something about a farmhouse on fire, abandoning the mission. A gunfight on the beach.

Someone was in the shit. She just hoped they would take it out on each other and not the girls.

Footsteps stomped down the gangway to their cabin. A wheel turned and the hatch opened.

Nikolas. The same man who'd locked them in there. His face pale and with the dazed look of a man who'd been punched in the face.

"Any of you bitches know first aid?"

"I do," Jaske said, before anyone else could answer. "I used to be a nurse."

13

"Come!" he barked.

She scurried out after him, grateful to escape.

4

BLACKWOOD NOTED THAT THE air reverberated. There was an echo to everything. A sonic boom in his ears. The muffled sonority of underwater.

It was definitely a submarine.

A floodlight pierced his brain. Migraine-heavy. He flinched away but couldn't move. The light stayed, glaring right down his eyeballs.

He gagged on the pungent waft of hydrogen peroxide.

No, a hospital. He was in a hospital. Not the submarine anymore. Though there had definitely been a submarine. It was important to remember that. Though he wasn't sure why it was important.

This was different. An unmistakable stench of death and disinfectant. This had to be a hospital.

He *had* been in a submarine, though.

Earlier.

Perhaps.

Or it had been a delirious dream.

There were more voices he couldn't understand, beyond the blinding light, and some he could understand.

"Give him another bag."

"Ease up on that."

"He's dead."

"Not this one. Nothing will kill him."

A wasp stung his abdomen with its vicious venom.

He tried to bat it away but his arm wouldn't move.

Persistent, the wasp stung again, and again and would not fly away.

He tried to cry out but his throat was sandpaper dry.

Paralyzed and mute. Was this death?

A woman's face loomed through the light and peered over him. Dark features, deep brown eyes, full sensuous lips. A nurse in a sweater, her dark hair pinned back.

There was no concern in her eyes. No feeling at all.

Someone pushed in over her shoulder. A familiar face. "Blackwood?" he said. "Fucking hell."

Pretke. Was that Pretke? What the hell was *he* doing here?

He hadn't seen Pretke since Iraq. A blazing car in Ramadi province. The midday desert sky turned black. Pretke had looked at it and said, "Boy, so this is what the first circle of Hell looks like."

The wasp stung him again and plunged a rusty knife into his guts.

A deep jolt of agony shuddered through Blackwood's bones and he plummeted into the black again.

5

Nikolas led her down the gangway, muttering, swearing under his breath.

From the men whose faces she caught she could see the devastation. Men who had just lost a major battle and had the fraught expressions of the defeated.

"The money's gone!" one of them yelled.

"What? All of it?"

"This is bullshit!"

Was it ten million? She'd heard that figure mentioned. The men talked all the time, like the girls couldn't hear. Perhaps because it was unimportant what they heard. They were going to be sold off anyway. Perhaps they were part of the ten million.

Nikolas led her down the long stretch of gangway until it opened out to a cramped mess hall where a body was laid out on one of the tables.

A man with a mop of dark hair and a forehead that was porcelain pale. Surely, he was dead. No. Dead men were not laid out on tables like that, hooked up to blood bags.

A couple of the Russians looked on, but it was the Norwegian they called Pretke who addressed her.

"You're a nurse?"

She nodded.

"Fix him," he said.

She stood over the man on the table. A pool of crimson stained his shoulder. He had been shot, that much was clear. She didn't know how to take a bullet out of someone. Her lie would fall at the first hurdle.

"Stitch him up," Pretke said.

On the next table were piled more blood bags and a scattering of medical supplies in white boxes. She rifled through them, reading the labels, as if assessing them with an expert eye. There was morphine. He would need that. Gauze. Cotton wool swabs. Sterilised thread. Sterilised needles. A sewing kit. Bandages, plasters, a tiny pair of scissors with a curled tip.

"You know how to sew, don't you?"

"I know," she said.

That was all it was. All she had to do was sew. It was a job that was too squeamish for them. Women's work.

She went to the stranger and looked him over, cutting open his t-shirt and peeling it off. She wiped his shoulder down with cotton swabs and assessed the extent of the wounding. A neat hole in his back and a messy exit wound at the front in the hollow below his collarbone. He'd been shot from behind.

She wondered if it had hit anything major, like an organ or artery. If it had, he would die, no matter how well she sewed him up.

She gave him morphine, pushing the tablets into his mouth and forcing him to drink them down, and then got to work on sewing him up. The first incision was the worst. She feared the needle wouldn't be strong enough to get through the skin, but it was big and thick and designed exactly for this.

Pretke looked away, squashed his cigarette under his boot and walked out. The Russian guards followed.

She had sewn it up as best she could but it was nothing like sewing a dress or repairing a blanket, nor even a moccasin. All of that she had done, and skilfully too. Human flesh was different. Her work was an angry gnarl of bloody thread. It would have looked better if she'd left it open. Now it was a bloody maw all tangled and discoloured at the edges.

She wiped the wound as best she could and covered it with a big square patch, sticking it down with strips of tape.

When it was done, Nikolas took her back to the bunk room and shoved her in with the girls.

They swarmed her with questions and she told them all she knew. Something had gone wrong. There was a stranger who'd been shot. That was all.

It seemed no time at all before the sub surfaced again.

"They're going to make a second attempt at the drugs deal," Mimmi said. "We *will* all be delivered to whoever is buying heroin and girls."

A boom that echoed through the sub sent a whimper of fright through the girls.

"They're unloading cargo onto a dock," Jaske said.

"We'll be next," Mimmi insisted. "We're the cargo."

Jaske fought the urge to slap her. She simply muttered an irritated *Shhhh!* like she was trying to listen.

The girls were moaning low now in an ululation of panic, like cows at the abattoir.

Footsteps clanged down the gangway. The girls cowered as the door pushed open.

Nikolas glowered at them. "Out!" he shouted. "Everyone! Out!"

The girls keened and wept but filed out down the gangway and towards the hatch.

Jaske took up the rear, the last one out, and Nikolas shoved her in the back with his gun. Not to hurry her — it was impossible to move faster as they were in a line waiting to climb out of the place — but to show his dominance, to take it out on her, someone, anyone.

She followed the last girl up the ladder and breathed the brackish air before she could see anything. As she came up and looked around, she let out an *oh* of surprise.

They were back on Hidra, on the same jetty where they'd loaded earlier.

Men with guns marched the girls back up the long craggy path to the compound where they'd lived for two weeks already. Two of the men carried the stranger on a stretcher.

Jaske tramped up the shale path to the compound and lowered her head to hide her smile. The men marched them back to the hut and as soon as the lock sounded, the girls exploded, chattering their questions over what this all meant.

"Why are we back on Hidra?"

"What happened out there?"

"What are they going to do with us now?"

They looked to Jaske for answers. She swallowed, knowing she didn't have any. "This is good," she said. "There's hope."

"We're back in our prison cell," Mimmi said.

"No. There's hope in this. If we're back on Hidra, the operation has failed and we're close to home again."

She took in their stupefied faces one by one.

"Don't you see?" she said. "There's a chance still."

6

LATER, MUCH LATER, BLACKWOOD blinked his eyes open. Someone had shot him in the head. They must have, because he could only see through one eye and his skull was an open wound, throbbing, nagging, pulsing. His brains must be oozing out of his skull and sliding down the side of his face.

He squinted at the mean, shabby room. A wooden hut with bunk beds. An oil heater hummed and creaked, emitting a pungent, claustrophobic stink, but it gave out no heat. It was still freezing.

He was tied to a drip, a needle in his arm. A blood pouch hanging from the top bunk. He craned his neck and tried to see the wound on his shoulder. A messy tangle of tape over a stained pad, where he'd been shot. Where Brand had shot him, before he'd killed Brand. The whole gang was dead.

Grove and Hicks and Crowe and Brand...

All of them.

And Blackwood's daughter had their money. He'd done it. He'd delivered retribution on them all.

He'd been happy to die, so it was inconvenient that he was still alive and in so much fucking pain.

What was the point of being alive now? He was an avenger who'd drunk from the skulls of his enemies. There were no more left to kill. There was nothing more to do.

The door opened and boots tramped in on bare floorboards. It wasn't the nurse, he was disappointed to note. It was Pretke.

The Norwegian pulled up a chair and scraped it across the floor and sat down, staring at Blackwood with a shake of his head and that same manic grin he'd had when he'd been staring at the first circle of Hell.

"Blackwood," he said. "You're alive. I'm sorry."

Blackwood tried to raise himself, but searing agony jack-knifed through his shoulder and he could only whisper, "Why?"

"Because you won't be alive for much longer."

Pretke said it like it was out of his hands. He shrugged as if to say, I don't like it but that's the way it is.

Blackwood sank back, his eyes rolling to the bunk above and the blood bag hanging from it.

If they were going to kill him, why were they keeping him alive at all?

And he realized it with a wave of nausea that flipped his soul like a fried egg in a hot pan.

They were nursing him back to health so they could torture him.

7

"THEIR LEADER," JASKE SAID. "The one called Rongstad. He's gone. I didn't see him on the jetty or the walk back to the compound, and there are two others I think are missing too."

"I didn't notice," said Zara.

"I thought I saw him," said Mimmi.

This was the way it always was. Always fucking Mimmi challenging her, trying to sway the girls against her. Jaske found her gaze rest on Noora, who always sided with whoever was dominant. She was a useful barometer for how things stood.

"Yes," said Noora. "I noticed Rongstad's absence too. It means he's dead; anyone can see that."

Jaske breathed a sigh of relief. Mimmi snorted derision.

The girls all chattered at the same time.

"What does it mean?"

"We'll be rescued, I know it."

"What's to become of us?"

"What do they want?"

"I don't know," Jaske said. "But being back here is good."

"Good?" Mimmi snorted. "You call this good?"

The girls looked between the two of them and Jaske could see some of them losing faith. They were starting to blame her for all of this. Sullen resentment beginning to curdle the fragile bond between them.

She didn't know if she had the spirit to win them over. She didn't know if she cared enough anymore.

"We're closer to home again. They took us away to sell us, and we're back where we started. That's better than being wherever they wanted to take us."

Mimmi shook her head, folding her arms. "They'll kill us now. I know it."

Another squall of panic rose and everything was lost in the swirl of chatter. Olivia and Sophie were weeping again.

Jaske stomped five paces across the hut and slapped Mimmi across her face.

The chatter cut dead. Mimmi reeled back, stung, and just stared.

"You know nothing. So shut your mouth."

Mimmi rubbed her reddened cheek and bared her teeth, ready to spit back a retort, when the lock rattled and everyone jumped. The girls shifted and Jaske noticed they were all behind her when the door opened.

Two men stepped in. The one leading was the man they called Pretke. He'd been the lieutenant, Jaske had noticed, so was now possibly the commanding officer.

"Nurse," he said, beckoning her. "Come with me."

Jaske filed out after them, again with a pang of guilt at escaping the girls. But it was better than being cooped up in this cabin. A fortnight of it beforehand had driven her insane. The thought of being sold off in Britain had almost been a relief, as at least she'd see the sky again. Even a foreign sky. She could tell herself that the sky over Britain was the same sky that was over the Finnmárku. But that was a lie too.

Just like the lie that she had been a nurse.

They crossed to the northernmost of the five huts that formed the compound. As she marched across, her boots trudging through shifting shingle, she scanned the horizon line of the escarpment that enclosed the compound. Over the other side, she knew, was a narrow channel of ice-cold sea and the mainland.

She dipped into the hut, between Pretke and the other man who fell in behind her.

It was the same as their own hut. A bunch of bunks lined along the long hut, but no one seemed to be billeted in this one, except for the stranger.

He was lying on the bottom bunk, a blood bag hooked up to him, hanging from the bunk above. On a table in the middle of the room, more blood bags and medical supplies.

The stretcher lay on the floor, buckled and forlorn, a pool of crimson staining its khaki.

Pretke waved in the stranger's direction then walked out. The other guard followed. They talked outside the hut in low voices for a while. She wouldn't be able to get out, not through the door. The windows were barred. Unless they moved, she had no chance.

The wounded man murmured, feverish, his face as pale as permafrost.

She maybe just had to clean him up. Take a look at the wound again. Put on a new dressing. More morphine. Something like that.

By the bags of blood was a scattering of medical supplies in white boxes. A sewing kit. A First Aid kit with bandages, plasters, a tiny pair of scissors with a curled tip.

She took the supplies to his bunk and began undressing his wound and dressing it up all over again while he mumbled.

She couldn't make out his words.

Yak, it sounded like. Had he said *Jaske,* her own name? No, *Jack.* And *I got you all.*

English. He was English.

Might he have been the contact at the British end, the one who arranged the deal? If the submarine had gone to Britain.

She leaned in close and whispered in his ear. "What's your name?"

He shook his head and rolled away.

She gripped his chin and held him firm and whispered again. "Tell me your name."

"Blackwood," he groaned.

It was not a name she'd heard them say. Brand, she had heard. It was said often. And Grove once, but no others.

She smeared the stitched-up wound with sterilised wipes. He groaned in pain. It must have stung him.

He would probably die.

Her stitching might kill him.

It didn't matter. He was just another of the men who would sell her like a can of beans.

She suppressed a pang of pity for him. It was best to harden herself. If she didn't get off this island and escape, all the men she would know from now on would buy her or sell her. If this one died, she didn't give a shit. It was one less in the world.

Still, she wiped his brow, and stuck on a clean patch before going to the door and stepping outside, where the guard was waiting. Pretke had gone.

"It's done," she said.

The guard led her back across the compound in the dusk light. It must be three in the afternoon. She scanned the horizon line again. Two hundred metres of running across shingle, up the escarpment, but once you were over the top, you had a clear run at the sea and escape. A short swim and you'd be free. Four hundred kilometres north-east was Oslo. Two thousand kilometres north was home. But she only needed to get across that narrow stretch of water and onto the mainland. The first town or village she could get to would mean salvation.

The problem was getting out of the hut, unseen, and then getting over that escarpment without them hearing her. If they could all be occupied with a noisy distraction, somehow.

The guard took her to the hut and shoved her inside.

He hadn't checked her at all. She shoved her hand in her jeans pocket and fondled the tiny pair of scissors.

8

BLACKWOOD WOKE TO THE sound of music. A thumping beat he didn't know. Some anonymous Euro techno beat. Voices, laughter, screaming revelry. A party resonating through the cabin walls.

He tried to work it out. He had botched up the gang's entire operation, but they were in retreat and were going to have a party. The after-defeat party to show the world they still had balls, to show themselves they were still alive. He'd seen that kind of thing before. It was a part of army life. Drink down your defeats and fuck the world.

He rolled onto his side, a sharp cataclysm of agony shuddering through his torso, so overwhelming he nearly blacked out.

He fiddled with the needle taped into his forearm, pulled it out and let it hang alongside the bed. A ball of blood beading on the white of his underarm.

He rolled over to the edge of the bunk and took in a sharp breath. He spilled over and fell to the floor with a brutal bang against the hard wood. He was surprised to find that an extreme movement like that resulted in the same amount of agony as twisting his body.

He dragged himself along the expanse of floorboard, crawling to the door, sucking in the pain, chanting a mantra: *gone, gone, gone, gone, gone.*

His ear against the door, he listened.

The music thumping through the night. Perhaps forty yards away. Difficult to tell. Another hut, certainly. Men's voices. Laughing. Drunk. Women too, but no laughter.

He thought he heard a woman crying.

Feet stamping. Drunken revelry.

He crawled back across the floor to a desk next to the oil heater and propped himself up against it, his head swimming. *Do not pass out, do not pass out, do not pass out.*

Empty blood bags scattered on the desk, packages of medical supplies. Morphine. He pressed a couple of tablets out of the blister pack and necked them. A First Aid kit. He rifled through it. Gauze, cotton wool swabs, sterilised thread, needles, bandages, plasters.

No scissors.

A drawer in the desk. He pulled it open, almost falling back. Held onto it, climbing, heaving himself up, his hand scrambling inside.

His fingers locked onto a narrow pipe. A pencil. He gripped it, closed the drawer, and fell back with a crash.

Not daring to breath, he lay still. They would come and find him there.

The music thumped on. No one came.

He crawled back to the bunk and climbed into his bed, stashing the pencil between the mattress and the bunk's frame.

Gasping, croaking like a ninety-year-old on his deathbed, he felt a wave of morphine bliss take him and fumbled with the needle to shove it back into his arm before he sank into its deep, dark embrace.

9

JASKE TRIED TO MAKE her body as small as possible, sinking into the corner of the room, hoping she might disappear into the shadows and they would forget about her. She necked a shot of vodka and held the empty glass, wondering if it might make a weapon.

The men were drunk and vicious, forcing the girls to dance. This was what it had come to. A macabre party with pushy, drunken men. Here was where they would turn from captors to rapists.

She couldn't protect these girls anymore. She had never been able to. It had never been possible. Who was she kidding? The men with guns always got what they wanted.

The chatter of abuse crackled between them, in Norwegian mostly and a couple barking Russian, slamming their vodka on the tables.

Mimmi squirmed in the embrace of Khryushka, the Russian Jaske feared the most, a sticky-fingered octopus, his tentacles all over her. Mimmi cried and trembled.

"Dance, you fucking bitch!" he yelled.

Another easy cheer for the boys.

He took Mimmi's wrists and she wrestled against him.

Jaske fought the urge to run across and smash her glass in his fucking eyeball, slit his throat with the broken shard. She couldn't protect these girls anymore, she couldn't protect herself.

Khryushka slapped Mimmi hard across the cheek and a wail of outrage shot up from the girls. And even herself. This was the moment they stepped over the line. They had been guards and now they would be rapists. The pretence of it being all just a party was about to evaporate.

Khryushka slammed Mimmi up against the wall and held her hair in his fist. He eyeballed her defiance as he stared into her face and she stared back into his. EyeThe outrage of it.

Jaske wanted a gun so she could shoot every fucking one of them.

She threw her vodka glass right at him and it smashed on the back of his skull.

He grunted and wheeled around.

The girls gasped surprise.

Khryushka felt the back of his head and examined the blood on his fingers. "You fucking bitch!" he growled.

And he tramped across the room at her, undoing his belt, drool slobbering from his slack mouth. A roar of encouragement went up from the men as he slammed into her. She heard herself scream as he grabbed her hair and smashed her down to the floor. She was on all fours and he was clawing at her buttons and zip.

Blindly fumbling for her pocket as he pulled her jeans down over her hips, she clasped the scissors. She couldn't reach behind her to stab him in the head, his weight pinning her down. His thigh. She could stab his thigh.

Someone shouted, "Stop that shit!"

Her fist closed on the scissors and she jerked her elbow back to get a good swipe — to plunge them into him with force.

A gunshot.

Screams.

Khryushka fell from her.

Jaske turned and scrambled to her feet. Khryushka was sitting away from her, glaring at Pretke, who had a gun in his face.

The music pounded on.

"What do you care about her," Khryushka said.

"We need the nurse," Pretke said.

Pretke flashed the gun away from Khryushka and shot the iPod dock. It shattered and fell to the floor in a tangle of twisted, singed ceramic.

He put his gun back to the head of Khryushka.

"Everyone fucking shut up," he yelled. "Beria is coming."

The name — whoever's it was — had an instantly sobering effect on the men, like an ice-bucket to their balls.

Khryushka rubbed his head and gulped and wiped the drool from his chin. There was no gun in his face now but he looked just as scared.

"Get these girls back to their hut," Pretke said.

The women clambered to the door and a few of the men followed them across to the hut in the black night.

Jaske stumbled into the hut and felt again the comforting outline of the pair of scissors in her pocket.

10

BLACKWOOD WOKE. THE MUSIC had stopped. His body was pleasantly numb, the after-wave of morphine still warm and blissful, like a hot bath you didn't want to get out of. But pain was there at the edges, like a creeping cold that would inevitably come and take hold.

The nurse came again. Footsteps tramping through shingle outside. The door opened. She came through carrying a tray. A guard let her in and stayed outside.

Blackwood let his hand fall to his side and into the gap between the mattress and the bunk edge. His fingers curled around the pencil lodged there.

The girl stood with her back against the door, staring, not moving. Then she edged over to the window and peeped outside. She shrank back. Someone had seen her.

The light was grey. Night falling or maybe it was dawn. It had been night when the music was playing.

"What time is it?" he croaked.

"Three," she said. "PM."

Soon it would be dark out there. That was good.

She came over with the tray and he smelled warm soup. "Can you sit?" she said.

His fingers left the pencil and he felt no pain as he shifted himself up the bed.

She put the tray on his lap. Tomato soup. A metal spoon. Another weapon he might use. Though they would check she left with it.

"Eat," she said.

"Can't move."

She looked at his hand and at the bowl and scowled. She pulled a chair over from the desk and sat beside the bunk. She spooned the soup into him. Her eyes on his. A thin bathwater that had a distant memory of chicken but was the greatest soup he'd ever tasted. His belly growled like a neglected dog he hadn't known was ravenous. For a while all he knew was the primal joy of gorging on sustenance. He cleaned the bowl and she put the spoon in the empty dish and the tray on her lap.

"Where are we?" he asked.

She looked him in the eyes for a long time and he wondered if she'd heard. "Hidra," she said.

"What's that?"

"An island. South of Norway. The gang brought us here after kidnapping us."

"Us?"

"You don't know?"

He shook his head.

That stare of hers again. Sizing him up. "There are ten girls here. I think they were taking us to Scotland to be part of some drugs deal."

That would make sense. A human trafficking sweetener as part of the deal. Each of those criminals who'd come had expected to leave with a case of heroin and a woman. He wished he'd killed them all over again.

"But the deal went wrong somehow."

Blackwood nodded. "I fucked it up." He wondered if she understood.

She looked over her shoulder, back at the door and bit her thumb. "There was a guy in charge here. Rongstad. He's missing now."

"I killed him," Blackwood said. "What's your name?"

She glared, sullen, as if working out if she could trust him. Then after a while said, "Jaske."

Almost like Jack. His daughter. Somewhere long gone with ten million in the boot of her car. He hoped. No one could know that.

"Why are you here?" she asked. "How are you involved in this shit?"

"I came to stop it."

"Liar," she said. "You can't stop anything. Look at you. You're barely alive."

"I need your help," he said.

"I could kill you with one little mistake." She nodded her head back to the table and its wreckage of blood bags and pharmacy packs. "What the fuck do I care about you?"

Rage at being imprisoned, held captive. Something had happened last night. Something that made her angrier. It was important to gain her trust. "Maybe you know I'm not one of them?"

She bit her lip and he could see it in her frown. A small part of her knew he wasn't one of them, but a large part of her couldn't trust any man ever again.

"They want you to nurse me back to health so they can torture me and find out what happened to their money."

"Their money?" she asked.

"A drugs deal. Ten million pounds. These guys were delivering the drugs. Twenty or more gang leaders came to a farmhouse to pay half a million each. I stopped them."

"You? Just you?"

"Yes. Just me."

"And where is this money?" Defiant, mocking, as if he were just some bloke bragging in a wine bar about his big deal at the office.

Could they have put her here to get it out of him; pump him for information: a kindly face to make him talk? If so, she was good. Way too good. "It's gone," he said. "They're all dead. All up in flames."

"You burned the money?"

His daughter had it. And she was somewhere they'd never find her. He hoped. He hadn't planned any of that, only the assault on the farmhouse, only making sure she'd be the only person left standing: the one who would drive away with it all.

But if he told this woman, they would find her. Better to let them think he knew enough to keep him alive, without ever letting them know enough. He could say it was still in the farmhouse. They wouldn't dare go there. It would be swarming with police now. If he told them that, they would kill him as he would be of no use to them anymore.

Just enough to make them think he knew where it was.

"No. The money's somewhere safe."

But he read it on her face. The pout of disgust. It was the wrong thing to say. It made him no different to the men out there.

She rose and the tray almost fell off her lap.

"And you're here to help?" she said. "What the hell can you do against them? You can barely walk. I could kill you myself by putting that pillow on your face. I could do it with one hand."

She went to the door and pulled it open. The guard out there sneered at her and she pushed past him and out, tramping across shingle. The guard pulled the door closed and locked it with a deadening click.

It was almost dark.

11

JASKE HAD ALMOST REACHED the mess hut to return the tray when she heard Khryushka's boots running behind her. She cowered as he reached her, fearing he might punch her in the back of the head, but he grabbed her arm and pulled her round. The tray fell, the bowl and spoon clattering to the hard ground.

His hot rancid breath in her face.

"What did he say?"

"What? Nothing."

"Don't lie to me, bitch. I heard you talking." He slammed her against the hut and her head cracked against clapboard. "Tell me what he said."

His claw nipping her arm. Sullen fury at the bitch who hit him with the glass. But there was something else, she could tell. It was this Beria guy that had them all scared. The mere mention of his name had smacked them into line like a pack of cowering dogs under a whip.

"He was asking where we are. What my name was."

"And the rest? Tell me or I swear I slit your throat. You think I won't slit your throat? You think anyone is gonna miss you, Sámi bitch?"

He wanted to slap her, punch her, rape her, just to show her who had the power, but he couldn't. Because he needed her. He wanted what she knew. So instead he simmered and raged.

She knew this didn't mean she was safe.

He would find a way to vent his frustration. Whoever Beria was, he wouldn't always have this hold over Khryushka. There would be a time, and then he would pounce and hit her hard.

She put her hand into her pocket and felt the outline of the scissors. Just to stab him in the throat, maybe. Smash the curled blade right into his jugular and watch his blood gush out of his neck, spraying the wall. Watch him drown in his own blood.

She came to.

She was back with his body pressed against her and his ashtray breath in her face. She'd fantasized about it too hard. Had actually zoned out to a sweet place where Russian thugs died spurting hot blood.

"He said he killed Rongstad. Him and everyone else."

She wanted to see it in his eyes. Fear. The threat of something greater than him.

Khryushka snarled and dragged her off. He was marching back to the prisoner's hut. "You're going to get it out of him. And if you can't do it, I'll fucking kill you both."

He hurled her towards the door. He wanted to get in Beria's good books, before he arrived. This was how much he feared him.

"And what if he kills you like he killed Rongstad?" she sneered.

To her surprise, he didn't smack her across the mouth. He laughed, his hand on the door handle for a moment. "We just put nearly two litres of blood into him. He's doing nothing."

He pushed her inside and she almost fell into the hut.

Blackwood turned in his bed, a quick glance, quicker than she expected.

Khryushka kicked the door closed behind him and pushed Jaske towards the bed. She fell into the wooden chair she'd left by the bunk. He dug in his trouser belt and

49

pulled out a pistol and put it to her head. Laughing at the man in the bed and switching to English.

"Hey, English. You like this girl, eh?"

The man looked from Khryushka to Jaske and didn't move, as if he was too weak to move, but she read it in his eyes — an alertness.

"You tell her everything, yeah? You tell her where the money?"

The man shook his head and swallowed, too weak to talk.

"You tell me, eh, or I blow her fucking brains out."

He pressed the gun harder against her skull and she cringed. All that stood between her and oblivion was the reflexes of a clumsy, drunken pig and the sweat on his finger.

The man croaked and nodded, beckoning Khryushka closer.

"The money... I'll tell you..."

Khryushka bent down. A moment of distraction and he might blow her brains all over the bunk.

"Fucking tell me where it is."

"It's... right... here."

A moment of startled confusion in Khryushka's eyes. What the fuck?

And then she was aware for an instant that the man was fumbling in the sheets.

A blur of movement.

The Russian fell back howling and dropped the gun.

A pencil sticking out of his eyeball.

The man leapt from the bed and shoved a ball of blanket in Khryushka's mouth. The howling became a muffled scream.

Jaske could only watch with fascination, frozen to the chair.

Khryushka was bucking, palpitating, his heels banging on the floorboards, his head rolling back and forth, mouth foaming. He might be vomiting, choking on his own vomit, she wasn't sure.

The man snatched up the pistol and in a flash of movement checked the clip. He dashed to the window and peered out, checking both ways, then put his hand on the door handle.

He looked back at her for an instant, as if thinking whether to take her with him, and then he was gone, closing the door quietly behind him.

It had happened in ten seconds.

She found she could stand. She went to the window and tried to see him in the dark. A blur running for the escarpment.

She should have run with him. This was her chance.

She went back to Khryushka and kneeled down beside him. His wide eyes blorting primal agony. The pencil quivering above his face.

She reached out and took it, as if she were about to write her signature on his eyeball.

She gripped it in her fist and slammed it down.

It stabbed through his brain with a squelch and he stopped palpitating.

12

Blackwood ran in a rapid ducking sprint into the darkness, his legs stiff, rebelling against him. A sharp pain flared across his shoulder. The morphine all worn out now. Soon his whole body would be one great spasm of pain, but all he could do was run.

His bare feet crunched shingle, at least quieter than boots, but would they hear the movement anyway? He dodged through the compound, getting his first sense of the layout, keeping true north in his mind. The sound of cutlery on tin plates in one hut. The guards eating. No one patrolling at all.

He skirted along another hut, its windows lit with an oil lamp glow. A low singing from inside. Women's voices. A folk song sung low, like a consoling lullaby.

Would Jaske sound the alarm? No. He thought not. She would cover for him as long as she could. His escaping would present her with a chance. He could tell the authorities about the girls being held on Hidra. He just had to get off this island.

Dodging through the huts, he came to the edge of the compound and paused, ready to break free.

He had to break out across an open stretch of land. Dangerously exposed but covered by darkness. The shale would make a noise underfoot. Draw attention.

He sucked in a deep breath and sprinted out through the blackness to the memory of the landscape.

The escarpment rising ahead. He hit the slope of it and felt its impact like a rugby tackle slamming into him.

The frozen ground numbed his feet and hands as he scrambled up the slope on all fours, the Makarov pistol in one hand making it awkward. Slowing to a crawl, his breaths short and sharp, each one burning his lungs.

But he was rising, and there was no sound of commotion behind, as much as he could hear over his own wheezing.

He scrambled to the summit and the roar of sea wind almost blew him back.

And then it came. Shouts echoing from hut to hut. Boots tramping on shale.

A gunshot.

It cracked on the horizon, ten feet to his left. Not a warning shot. Not a shot to raise the alarm. They had seen him.

He jumped over and found himself scrambling falling flying down the other side of the hill in a mad helter-skelter tumble.

He fell at the bottom in a heap and wanted to lie down and sleep forever. So easy to give himself up to the cold ground.

He pushed himself up, raging through gritted teeth, and peered through the blackness ahead. A dark expanse of water and the dim outline of mainland beyond it. He guessed it was maybe half a mile across. Swimming in ice cold water. He might cramp up and drown halfway, or go into shock at the temperature.

But it was either swim or be killed.

He looked both ways, up and down the stretch of coastline.

They would come over the hill straight for where he'd last been seen. That would be the obvious point of chase.

And they would think he'd head east, away from the jetty and the submarine docked there.

Head towards the danger. They wouldn't expect that. Do the opposite.

He jerked left and headed straight for the jetty where they'd docked.

He darted along the shoreline, his feet thumping soft heather. Nice and quiet.

Heart burning, shoulder stinging. That red-hot poker shoved into his wound again, being twisted.

He heard them come over the hill way back, exactly where he'd come over. They ran down the steep slope, clattering and falling. At least one of them, maybe two, tripped and went headlong down the shingle slope. A gunshot went off. Probably an accident.

They were amateurs. Maybe drunk.

Blackwood darted on, taking the bend of shore till the shape of the jetty emerged. The fat outline of the submarine.

The voices were fading. They were doing exactly what he'd expected. They were pursuing him east. A machine gun rattled in the night.

He stumbled to a halt twenty yards short of the jetty and doubled over. A sharp pain through his chest that took his breath from his lungs and left him gasping.

He half ran, half crawled to the jetty and ducked into its shadow.

No sign of a boat of any kind. He didn't think he could steal a submarine. So he would have to swim for it. Another flare of pain fireworked through him at the thought.

He had to steel himself and plunge in. It was the only way.

A shuffling sound.

He jerked to his left, raising the Makarov.

A figure loomed out of the jetty's shadow to his side.

"Don't move."

An unmistakable Russian accent.

The crack of a pistol being cocked. A Makarov, like his own.

The cold press of the barrel to his temple.

Blackwood sank to his knees, fighting for breath. He was gulping paroxysms, palpitating, and didn't know if he was laughing or crying.

He fell to the ground and the unconsciousness that greeted him was a relief.

13

PRETKE RAN TO THE jetty when he heard the gunshot echo. The men had stormed off over the escarpment. Some had circled off to the east. There had been no order to it. Just a random pack of dogs on the chase. No real military training.

Beria had walked off in the opposite direction, quite calmly, as if strolling off to the shower hut in the morning. In the direction of the jetty. Surely, he hadn't thought Blackwood would head there?

Pretke ran down the shingle slope in the dark, till he could see the jetty and the submarine silhouetted by moonlight on the black water.

Two figures down off the jetty. Blackwood on the floor. Beria standing over him pointing a gun to his head. There had been no shot, though. He hadn't killed him yet.

How had Beria known Blackwood would run this way?

Pretke swallowed down an indigestible wad of fear. There was something inhuman about Beria. Everyone had a sixth sense, an intuition, in varying degrees, it was normal. Every soldier had it when they sensed they were in the enemy's scope and just a trigger away from death. Your gran had it when she knew you were going to call. Beria had more than that, a seventh sense, like he was inside your head and knew what you would do before you did it.

But as terrifying as he was, Pretke thought, at least Beria wasn't Nepravda.

Pretke tramped to them, the shale alerting them to his approach over the hissing roar of the sea wind. Neither man looked.

Would he just put a bullet in Blackwood's head? Like a lunatic.

"Don't kill him," Pretke said. "He knows where the money is."

Beria turned and even in the darkness, his face half in shadow, Pretke sensed the Russian looked at him like he was a shit-stained imbecile who'd wandered into a cabinet meeting.

More footsteps came running from behind and from along the coastline, some of the men finally understanding that Blackwood hadn't run the other way. They clustered and formed a half-circle, an amphitheatre with an impromptu audience for an unbilled entertainment, with the unease of people who were unsure if they would be part of the show.

"Take him back," Beria said.

A few of the men rushed forward to take Blackwood's limbs. They hoisted him up and ran with him suspended between them, face down, a dead deer ready for dismemberment.

They stomped back to the compound and no one said anything but for the shouts in the distance, calling the men back, the fools who were still scouring other parts of the island.

They dumped Blackwood back in his bed, stepping over Khryushka's dead body. Blackwood had rammed a pencil through his eye. A fucking pencil.

Pretke lowered his face to hide the smirk of satisfaction. Khryushka had been a pain in the balls — a useless boor, the type you had on board for violence — a lump hammer on a surgeon's table. The moron's out-of-control antics the previous night had made Pretke fear he was losing control almost as soon as he'd taken command. He'd whipped the attack dogs into line with the threat of Beria's arrival, but he knew it was only a matter of time before the dogs turned on him.

Blackwood had almost done him a favour in disposing of the yappiest dog in the pack. And it was one less Russian too, and that was a relief.

No. That was wrong. Beria had arrived. And Beria was twice as scary as Khryushka. The lump hammer had been replaced by a Saiga-12 shotgun.

"Get this one out of here," Beria said. "Go and bury him somewhere."

He waved his Makarov vaguely in the direction of outside. Somewhere. Anywhere.

The four who'd carried Blackwood in now hauled Khryushka out, happy to be out of this theatre, away from this show where the actors could round on the audience at any moment.

Blackwood lay panting on the bunk, out of it — lucky, in a way — and Pretke thought again of the incredible coincidence of it all. Here was John Blackwood. From his own unit. From the Iraq operation. Too much of a coincidence.

A few of the men hovered uneasily in the hut. The others were outside. The lucky ones.

Beria paced the hut, stepping through the pool of blood on the floor, because he didn't notice, or perhaps to show he didn't care.

"And what the fuck are we to do now?" he said.

The men looked to one another, wondering if they should answer. Then they looked to Pretke.

He wasn't sure what Beria meant or if he was talking to himself. "I think we go back to Macduff. Hit it hard. Follow the trail to the money." He almost laughed after the words had left his lips. Here he was, talking like a Russian. Win at all cost. Run into the fire screaming for victory.

"The story is all over the news," Beria said. "The location is swarming with police and media. They're reporting a burning farmhouse. Talk of explosions, drugs gangs shooting up a small fishing village. Half the world is watching."

"You think we should retreat?"

"I think our money isn't even there."

"So, yes. Find out from him where it is and then go get it. Quickly. We're wasting time here." Pretke swallowed, gulping down his insubordination.

A commotion outside was sweet relief from Beria's glare. Someone shoved the girl in. The Sámi girl he'd told to nurse Blackwood. She'd been there when it happened.

Eager to show that he was in charge and had not failed, Pretke stepped forward. "You. What did he say? Where's the money?"

She looked from him to Beria and shook her head.

Beria smiled and circled her, taking over.

Pretke felt himself shrinking. He wasn't the main character in this drama anymore. He had lost control.

"Be aware that we know everything you talk about," Beria said. "I already know what he told you. What I don't know is if I can trust you to tell me the truth. I like to know who will lie to me. Are you a liar, girl?"

She shook her head.

Pretke sensed something come off her. Normally, with girls like this, little bitches who thought they could lie and dissemble, they quaked and blurted out the truth and you could smell the fear off them, like they'd pissed their knickers. But this girl burned defiance. Almost like she didn't care what he did to her. Like he could put a bullet in her brain and she would fall to the floor saying *fuck you*.

"Did he tell you where the money is?"

She shook her head.

"Then he's no use to us. Kill him."

And there was concern in her eyes now. Surprise and then that little spark of fear.

"He said he knows where it is."

Beria turned on her, circled her again, sniffing out the truth. "He told you this? Why would he tell you this?"

"He said you wanted me to nurse him back to health so you could torture him to find out where the money was. That it was a drugs deal gone wrong. He said he killed Rongstad and everyone else. He said he's going to kill all of you too."

And there it was. Beria flushed. Two little muzzle flares of irritation lit his cheeks. Anger. Blackwood had boasted to this girl and told her everything.

Beria said nothing. He turned and stomped out of the hut. The door slammed and flapped open again.

The girl's face stayed immobile, frozen, but Pretke thought he caught a little something in her eyes. A smile.

14

JASKE DIDN'T KNOW IF she was supposed to go back to the girls' hut or stay and tend to the Englishman.

Pretke barked some orders to his men, about how he wanted two of them in the hut at all times, armed, seated either side of the door with a good ten yards distance between them and the bunk. They should never go anywhere near the prisoner. Let the girl do that.

"If he gets up and approaches you in any way, shoot him." Pretke turned to her and barked, "See to his wounds and then go back to your hut."

He stormed out.

Two of the men stayed and sat against the wall, Kalashnikovs across their chest. She read the fear in their eyes. They'd seen what he'd done to the pig, Khryushka.

Just this sleeping, dying man in a bunk.

She got to work tending to him. His feet were congealed with mud and blood. She heated a kettle on the stove and poured half out into a bowl before it boiled. Just enough tepid water to wash the blood and mud off his feet and ascertain the damage. As she wiped them clean, she saw that his feet were scarred and bloody but not blue. The danger was frostbite. He might lose them. She didn't fancy having to hacksaw his feet off. Surely, they wouldn't ask her to operate on him. Surely, if it came to that, they would just let him die.

She wasn't sure how she felt about that. This man might be someone who could help.

He had promised to kill all the men.

But he had killed one and run away.

The swift, brutal execution of the pig still resonated in her breast. The merciless speed of it. The pig was alive, snorting and shitting all over you, and then in a moment he squealed and died.

No. That wasn't right. It wasn't Blackwood who had killed the pig. He'd only stuck the pencil in his eye, reduced him to a flailing piece of wreckage. It was Jaske who'd killed him. Shoving the pencil through his rotten fucking brain and watching the life leave his body. An abattoir electric bolt to the head that had extinguished him.

Blackwood hadn't killed the man. She had.

She glanced at the guards sitting either side of the door, already bored. Neither of them knew she'd killed one of them. They didn't suspect, and that made it all the easier for her to kill another.

She smoothed her palms along her jeans and felt the ridge of the scissors in her pocket.

She pulled Blackwood's shirt off and examined his shoulder. There was the wound she'd sewn up herself, her messy tangle of bloody thread, but it seemed there were no new wounds from the escape. He hadn't been shot and they hadn't beaten him again.

His breathing was deep and distant, like he was in a coma, but he flinched when her fingers brushed the wound.

She traced her fingertips over the contours of his body. There were other scars, old scars, silver ridges long since healed over, and scarlet cuts, fresher. There were several bruises, livid purple, and a hole below his collar bone on the other side. A burn, as if someone had stubbed out a cigar, used him as an ashtray.

He was wreckage. Walking wounded.

What could he possibly do to help her?

Perhaps he was as full of shit as the rest of these men. All of them.

Except Beria, she thought. He was the only man on the island you could expect to back up his talk. Beria wasn't a man, though, more of a shark in a uniform. Hard to read. He had a cold stone face that gave away nothing, but Jaske but Jaske had seen how the others lowered their heads and backed away. It had been there in the air between them, like a blast of body odour. Everyone tried to ignore it, but their faces curdled a little at the stench of it.

She bandaged Blackwood's feet, as much to keep them warm as anything else, and cleaned his hands of blood and grime, wiped him down, made him look new. He opened his eyes, once, an animal alert to predators, then closed them again, as if he'd assessed the danger and was happy he was safe. He might have done it in his sleep, or he might be pretending. She had no idea.

She went through the medical supplies again and read the box of morphine.

Sevredol 50 mg.
Film-coated tablets
morphine sulphate.

Blister packs of blue tablets. She popped one out and pushed it into his mouth, held his head up and put a tin cup of water to his lips. He drank and swallowed as if he sensed he would need more of it. He had at least earned some relief from pain.

She wondered if she should steal some for herself. Some escape from all of this. A fleeting thought. She let it float away on the wind and forgot about it.

There was nothing more to do. She turned to the guards and nodded.

One of them reached to his side and rapped on the door.

A guard standing outside opened the door.

She walked out and back across to the women's hut and before she got there she wished she had made up an excuse to stay longer with him.

15

BERIA STOMPED ACROSS SHALE to the edge of the compound and looked out at the rise of the escarpment ahead, a great wall that seemed to shield the island from the mainland just over that narrow strip of sea. The escarpment was steep and vast, a treacherous wall of sharp rocks, and this man Blackwood had scaled it barefoot like it was a garden hedge.

He turned to see the men hovering, awaiting orders. None of them knew what they were doing.

A compound shielded from the mainland by the escarpment on a tiny, uninhabited piece of rock. It was perfect. It had all been perfect. And now it was shit.

Beyond the cluster of men, Pretke emerged from the prisoner's hut, saw them and couldn't stop himself from glancing at the ground before trudging across to them, head up, back straight. Military bearing. One of the few actual soldiers on this operation. There were Beria's own Russian soldiers, but they were soft and few of them had seen action. Only Khryushka had seen action. In Chechnya. The rest were just boys in uniform who'd spent their national service sitting in a remote outpost shipping contraband across a border.

The Norwegians in the crew were all low-level criminals. And when he looked at it honestly, no different to his own men. None of them had military experience. Only Rongstad, who was dead.

And Pretke.

Beria found himself smiling. Two men on each side who'd seen war, and one on each side was dead. A Russian and a Norwegian. Only two real soldiers left standing.

Pretke came up to him and slouched to a stop.

"How has this happened?" Beria said.

"I've been involved in this for a year of planning," Pretke said, "and didn't hear Blackwood's name mentioned once. It would have come up if Rongstad had taken Blackwood on board. I'm sure of it."

"You know him."

Pretke gulped and nodded and glanced at the ground again. "Iraq. He was... a member of an elite group. Special operations. Rongstad knew him too."

"You think Rongstad involved him in this."

"Maybe. They knew each other from Iraq."

"Why would Rongstad involve this man Blackwood in this operation, without telling anyone?"

Pretke shrugged. "Maybe he bragged about it to him and Blackwood got the idea to storm in to take the money for himself."

And got shot and ended up in the boat that had transported the drugs to the shore. It was all such a bizarre sequence of events that stood out in stark contrast to the carefully planned military operation they had prepared. But it was like most carefully planned military operations he'd seen: once in motion, they were hijacked by the absurd. Fate had a grim sense of humour.

"Rongstad must have involved Blackwood somehow," Pretke said. "And Blackwood betrayed him. That's the only explanation."

Beria rubbed his fist, an overwhelming urge to punch Pretke's face in. Punch it till he'd turned his stupid face to steak. These fucking Norwegians had fucked it all up.

His phone bleeped. He dug it from his pocket with a qualm of dread.

A message from *Nepravda*.

Instinctively, he turned, so no one would read his face.

He took a breath and thumbed the message to read the whole of it. The instructions were clear. But for a moment he entertained the fantasy of dismissing them. They were not orders. Nepravda did not outrank him. He wasn't even an officer. Not a Russian. A mere foreign advisor. These were merely tactical suggestions. But they might as well have come from the Tsar's lunatic son.

The message ended with the words: *They have failed. The one called Blackwood. Bring him back. And the girls.*

Beria burned with anger. This whole operation had been fucked up by a single man. Nepravda had called it back in, and that meant failure.

He turned and shouted, "Pack up everything. Get the women and the prisoner onto the submarine. We're leaving. Now!"

Pretke jumped to the order and turned to the men. He opened his mouth as if about to repeat the order.

"Not you."

"What?"

"You're staying here."

He read it in Pretke's face. The little smile of hope. That he had persuaded Beria to go after the money and not retreat.

Beria took out his Makarov, cocked it.

And the hope fell from Pretke's face.

The explosion made them all jump.

Pretke fell to the floor, crimson spurting from his head.

"You and you," he said, pointing to two of the closest crew members, both Norwegians. "Bury this fucking idiot right here."

Beria stomped off towards the submarine, kicking up a shower of shale as he marched. Pretke lay dead, but Beria didn't feel any less angry.

16

BLACKWOOD FLINCHED AWAKE.

A single gunshot out there, and the echo bouncing back off the escarpment. He was back in the bunk. He raised his head and felt no pain, just the pleasant morphine fog. The same hut. His feet bandaged.

Two guards, one sitting either side of the door. Kalashnikovs across their chest. They sat up a little, wary.

He'd escaped and been caught. The Russian. The only intelligent one of the entire mob. He hadn't shot him.

Footsteps running in the shale outside. Lots of them. Running in different directions. Several heading right for this hut.

The door flew open and the guards shot up out of their chairs. Orders barked in Norwegian. They laid the limp stretcher on the floor beside the bunk.

They weren't going to shoot him. No. Of course not. They wanted the money still.

Two of them hoisted him off the bed and dumped him onto the stretcher. One of them scraped all of the medical supplies off the table and into a bag. In a flash, they were bumping him outside. The cold air hit him and the harsh glare of daylight. He craned his neck to see as much as he could.

Men running everywhere, clearing the camp. They were leading the girls out and a few of them shrieked. At the centre of this commotion, something odd: a couple of men digging a hole. As they bumped past with the stretcher, Blackwood saw the body prone on the ground, the pool of blood from the skull, and recognized Pretke. That had been the single shot. The Russian had killed him. For his failure. For what Blackwood had done to them all.

They continued on down the slope, heading for the jetty and the submarine.

The random chaos of flight formed into a single file and he remembered how they'd arrived this way.

They got him onto the sub and took him off the stretcher. They dumped him on someone's back and carried him to a berth where they threw him onto a bunk and left the bag of medical supplies.

Boots tramped along the metal gangways, the frantic business of preparation. His bunk door opened, someone shoved the girl in and shut the door on them.

"What's happening?"

She tucked her hair behind her ear and glared, as if surprised to find him alive. "We're going back. They're taking us back."

Disbelief and a little joy. Hope in her voice.

"Where is back?" he asked.

"To the Finnmárku. The Russian part, where they took us first."

"We're going to Russia?"

She nodded. "There's a military base there just over the border with Norway. But to us, either side of it is Sámi land. We don't see their borders. They're taking us back home."

"I don't think that's the idea," Blackwood said.

She slumped onto the bunk, sitting by his feet. "I know, but better than being here. If we're close to home, close to where they first took us, there's a chance. In twenty hours, we'll be there."

Shouts echoing outside. Orders in Russian. Clanking on the hull. They were getting ready to dive.

"The Russian who caught me," Blackwood said. "Who is he?"

"Beria," she said. "I don't know who he is but I know they're all scared of him."

The engines roared into life and reverberated through the sub. His teeth rattled with the hum. And then the unmistakable feeling that they had set off.

They would push out from shore and then dive once they were out to sea.

Blackwood pondered what was ahead. Beria was taking them back to Russia. Blackwood was in deep now. They weren't going back for a debrief. It was to reassess and re-arm and figure out how to retrieve the money. And that would involve a great deal of torture on the only person who knew where it might be.

He had to pretend to be alive enough to be useful, but too weak for torture. A tightrope walk. Beria would have him shot in an instant if he thought he was no longer useful, and Blackwood was too weak to fight his way out of this. He needed time to get his strength back.

He wasn't sure twenty hours would be enough.

17

Beria stormed into his bunk and fought the urge to punch the wall. There were no walls in a submarine you could punch. He threw off his greatcoat and fur hat, kicked off his boots and reached for the bottle of Stolichnaya. Slumping on the bunk, he knocked back a couple of shots and lit a cigarette.

He had smoked in submarines when he'd first started, usually in the back of the engine room. They said the air filtration was supposed to be the best on submarines. Then the order had come through forbidding it. Some shitty study found the scrubbers and burners only removed half the nicotine from the air and recirculated the carcinogens. He wished he could have shot the fucking academic who'd shit out that study.

But fuck it and fuck that study. This wasn't a navy submarine. It was a mafia boat and he was head of the mafia.

He could smoke in the sub if he wanted and he'd stub his cigarette out in the eye of any fucker who told him not to.

He poured more vodka and felt his neck loosen. Twenty hours of this. It was best to lose oneself. Wipe oneself out. Halfway through this bottle, the annoying details of this failed mission would stop circling behind his eyes.

The mission had failed. The Norwegians had failed. Now they had to retreat and take the assets with them. They could still traffick the girls. They could torture the Englishman at their leisure and get the information. Namely, the location of ten million. And Beria could make it clear to his superiors that he was still in line.

And there was Nepravda too. His shadowy involvement somewhere between the government and its dark operations, and Beria and his corrupt sideline.

He poured another generous shot of vodka, spilling some of it across his chest. Sloshing it back. He wiped his face and sucked his fingers.

Twenty more hours in this tin can. But what awaited him at the other end was not freedom, nor home, even though it should have been those things. What awaited him was the man they codenamed Nepravda.

A qualm of shame. That moment the message had come through and Beria had turned from those men. Not so they couldn't read his face, but so they wouldn't see the fear written there.

The moment played again and again in his mind. When he had taken a deep breath and thumbed the message to read the whole of it, his skin crawling. Every time he saw a message from Nepravda, it was like a tarantula had somehow learned how to text you.

Nepravda was the only man he feared. Him and the tsar.

He knocked back two more shots and slunk back, the ceiling blurring above. The cigarette fell from his limp hand to the bunk floor.

He turned over and watched it on the grey metal deck, watched its glowing tip slowly die, a thread of blue smoke curling up to be lost before it reached the ceiling. Like that burning farmhouse. Their operation going up in smoke.

The Englishman knew where it was. He would get the information out of him then shoot him in the head and dump him somewhere in the vastness of the tundra.

He didn't know if that would be enough.

He rolled off the bunk and slammed to the metal floor. Leapt up. Dizzy for a moment, he reeled and his hands found the door to hold him up.

He yanked the door open and yelled.

One of the men came running and stopped, startled. He must look a state. Nothing like the man who'd stepped aboard an hour ago.

"Get one of the girls and bring her here," he said.

"Which one, sir?"

"Any fucking one."

The man ran off and Beria staggered back, undoing his belt and slumped onto his bunk.

18

The Chinook flew in low towards Linhammar under cover of a blizzard. The cockpit screen that the four-man crew looked through was a sheet of white. How the hell did they know where they were going?

The private, the youngest of the four-man patrol in the passenger hold, checked the faces of his comrades for fear, but they were as easy and nonchalant as they were in the mess hall. He swallowed the sliver of doubt and tried to look as confident as they did.

Only one face mirrored his fear back to him, like he was infectious and could spread it: the scout attached to their patrol. A kid barely out of school, dressed in Norwegian army camouflage.

"So what's his story?" Haines said. "He's said nowt all this mission."

83

"He's a Sámi," said Benson. "They're like the red Indians round here. They live in wigwams and herd reindeers."

"I think they live in houses now," Maxwell corrected, shaking his head with disdain.

Haines sneered, a dog with a bone who wasn't about to let go. "So he's a savage, then."

"Careful, Haines, he'll scalp you if you turn your back on him."

"We don't herd reindeer," the scout said. "We follow them."

"Ooooh, he's got a voice."

"And he speaks English."

"He's here," said Maxwell, "because the Sámi are the only ones who know this land. You see, it's been disputed for a century or more."

"So if we get lost, Little Plum here's gonna save us?"

"That's right," said the scout. "Because you're in my country now."

He wasn't scared at all, this boy, now that you got a really good look at him. There was a stillness to him that you might take for shyness or fear, but he was solid and he didn't give two fucks about this patrol of Brit soldiers.

Benson leaned forward with sudden menace. "It ain't yours, pal. You lost it to everyone who came and fancied a piece. Norway, Russia, Sweden. You even let fucking Finland take a bite. How shit are you that you let the Finns fuck you over?"

Benson and Haines cackled. Maxwell shook his head but grinned along with them.

The private smiled too. It didn't pay to be out of step with your patrol buddies. You did what they did, even if what they did was bully some scout who, if the slightest thing went wrong, would be the native in charge; the man who could get you home.

The scout closed his eyes for a moment, like he was taking a deep breath or counting to ten. Maybe he was going to pull out some Kung Fu shit, who knew.

It didn't bother Haines and the others. They carried on laughing with their easy barrack room bullying bravado. Another easy laugh for the lads.

He'd expected better in the Pathfinders. A bit of intelligence. They were supposed to be sharp instruments. This man was part of their unit and if anything went wrong, he'd be their way out of trouble — any fool could see that.

Maxwell rabbited on about the history of the terrain, like he'd done while they were on the ground erecting their microwave receiver under cover of the war games operation going on — a secret patrol sneaking over the border to put up a spy dish between two towers. *We'll pick up every word that passes through this space. Clock all the traffic between Moscow and Murmansk.*

"The Norway-Russia border has always been fluid," Maxwell said. "There's just no way to construct a border. And another problem is the human population. These guys."

He pointed to the scout.

"The local population are Laplanders. Nomadic people whose tradition means they travel where they like either side of that artificial border."

"That right, Little Plum? You pitch your wigwam anywhere you like?"

"We're not called Laplanders," the scout said. "We're *Sámi*. And my name is Viggu."

"Did he say my name is *fuck you?*"

Laughter.

"Good comeback."

"Nice one, Fuckyou."

Even Haines broke into a smile and laughed with the others.

"There have been a number of near misses over the years," Maxwell went on. "Any westerner wandering into this region could cause tension to kick off rather nastily. Which is why we need to be discreet. Get them and get out."

The private caught the smirk that passed between Haines and Benson. They didn't want it to be quiet or discreet. They wanted a ruck.

"That Korean airliner shot down recently. That was here. There's been a sort of local agreement in place. If your air patrol comes down on the wrong side, say in weather like this, your crew is allowed to walk back over by 72 hours or there'll be hell to pay. This land is littered with wrecks, going right back to World War Two. That's why it's called the German Peninsula."

"You see," said Benson, staring at the scout. "The Krauts took it as well."

The scout didn't respond.

The pilot called back. "We're due to land!"

"Right, men," said Maxwell. "You know what to do. No messing about. Just retrieve and retreat."

A Norwegian patrol flight somewhere down there in the blizzard, waiting to be rescued before the Russians took them. It was all so simple.

Except no one had a right to be here.

The Chinook swooped and the private felt his belly lurch. They landed with a bump and in moments the door was open and they jumped out, crouch running into the blizzard under the rotating blades.

He could see nothing but a haze of white. Maxwell pointed the way and moved north-north-west, Benson and Haines following, the scout behind them and the private bringing up the rear.

They ran some fifty yards before a shape loomed out of the snow fog. The Norwegian plane. The private checked the path that led to it, where it had gouged a road through the snow as it crash landed.

Figures emerged from the stricken plane. The Norwegian crew.

Maxwell had a hurried conflab. The Norwegians had a stack of cases to bring with them. Whatever it was, they didn't want to leave it here behind Russian lines. Maxwell waved an arm towards the Chinook, barely visible through the storm. The Norwegians took their flight cases, two men to a case.

This would hold things up. They would need two or more trips. It wasn't a straight in and out job anymore.

The private scanned the horizon he couldn't see, just a blur of stark white, dizzying, when you weren't sure if you were looking at the land or the sky.

Something out there, in the howl of the storm, the persistent whine of a mosquito. Impossible in this place. No.

It broke through the sky with a great bang. A jet fighter. Bearing down on them. With a hiss of venom, two streamers launched.

The private dived into snow and only heard the impact, like God had punched a hole through the sky.

When he looked up, the great arm of the plane was in the air, like a swimmer frozen mid-stroke, flame and smoke all around.

And bodies. Red meat scattered all over.

Everyone dead.

He lay paralyzed. A voice telling him to run. But he couldn't move.

The Chinook roared. They were preparing to flee.

He had less than a minute to fight his way through the snow and jump on board before...

A lone figure running through the white haze. Someone had survived. The scout?

The whine of the jet returning. It was coming in for another pass.

He tracked it through the white haze. An F-16.

One of ours. What the fuck are they doing?

He screamed in protest. A helpless child.

The jet swooped in again, coming for him, only him. This was it.

It spat its venom with a great hiss. A missile left a trail of vapour. It arced over home.

The Chinook exploded in a great ball of flame and disintegrated.

The F-16 swooped away. He caught its tail insignia. A single grey star circled on a bar of stripes.

He checked his legs, afraid he would feel nothing. Afraid his legs were gone. No. Still intact. He punched his thigh and jumped up.

Praying that the jet didn't return for another swoop.

But it droned off into the storm and was gone.

He was out here on his own.

He scanned the terrain, all 360 degrees of it. A hill fort to the south. What looked like abandoned buildings.

He could run there for cover, but wouldn't that be the obvious place you'd look?

A Russian patrol would be here any second.

No. The best thing to do would be to strike for home.

He took out his compass. That way was west.

As far as he could see, it was bleak, open terrain, but he knew there were vast stretches of forest between here and the border. If he could get to them quickly, he would be hidden.

He turned from the smouldering wreck and ran. Sprinting through deep snow, his frantic breath clouding around his face.

It was about a hundred kilometres to the border, and no guide to lead the way. At least there was no real border. At least there was that.

One thing burned into his mind as he ran, burned his soul and put anger in his step: the jet that had come and shot them all to shit, was a US plane.

19

JASKE TENDED TO THE Englishman as much as she could. He fell into a deep sleep and she sat and stared at him for a long while. She was avoiding going back to the bunk. She registered this, nodded, noting this and assessing why she was doing it. She didn't want to be in the company of the girls again. This man was a welcome escape from them.

She stood and went to the door, forcing herself to step through it.

Out in the corridor, one of the men sat in a chair. He sneered. One of the Norwegians. Orvik was his name. Something about his raw glare of hatred. She'd seen it before in men who hated women and hated anyone who didn't share their skin colour. Just hated everyone who wasn't them. He was nothing new.

"*Jævla fitte,*" he growled.

Jaske cringed at the insult. You had to walk around them, avoid them, make yourself look smaller, present no threat to them — and that meant to seem meek — any indication of independence was a mortal threat to their sense of superiority.

She lowered her eyes and slunk down the corridor to the bunk room where the women were held. Another man sitting guard down there.

She kept her eyes on the floor and pushed open the door, closing it behind her.

The women looked up, some in terror, some in expectation, and she saw the relief when it was only her, one of them, not a man, one of the others.

The bunk room was cramped and dirty and meant for only ten crewmen, a fraction of the size of the hut they'd stayed in for three weeks. That seemed palatial now. They were two to a bunk, but it didn't matter to the men because this was just a 20-hour shuttle to someplace else. The women were dirty and crying.

Jaske felt a hard lump of anger swell in her throat and tried to swallow it. The indignity of it.

"We'll be back home soon, girls," she said.

"Home?" Mimmi sneered. Of course it was Mimmi. It was always Mimmi. "We could be going anywhere."

"We're going back to where they set off. Vayda-Guba."

"And how do you know?"

"I heard the men talking of it."

"You know more than any of us. Maybe you're one of them. Maybe you set us up?"

Mimmi looked to the others for support, and Jaske saw it in their faces. Some of them nodded and glared, burning with resentment. Others looked at the floor.

All the time she'd been away with Blackwood, Mimmi had been shooting her mouth off, turning them all against her. It was plain to see.

She looked for the right words to say, but the only thing that came out was, "Don't be stupid."

"We were all on your stupid excursion," Mimmi yelled. "It was almost like you planned it."

"Mimmi, I'm trying to get us home. Get us free."

"And what the fuck are you doing while they rape us? Sitting with the enemies."

"No one has been raped."

"They took Helve."

She looked around their faces. Yes, Helve was gone. Jaske wanted to say something, something to appease them, put them at ease, give them the hope that she felt. But her throat froze and she stammered. It had finally happened. It had always been a matter of time. Now the men would taste the merchandise. Because the deal had failed. The Englishman had destroyed their deal.

"I have hope," she said. "We're going back to where we started and it stands to reason that there's a chance of escape."

"You've been saying this all the time," Mimmi said, "and we are no nearer to that."

Jaske was about to tell them the Englishman was going to help them. But they had no reason to trust him and she could imagine their disdain if the words left her lips. And besides, there was another disturbing thought. If she told them what she thought of the Englishman, there was no telling if one of them might relay that information to the men. They might do it accidentally. They might use it to bargain for favourable treatment. It was possible. The women were already splitting apart and desperate to make any kind of pact to save themselves at the expense of the others. She couldn't trust them anymore.

"It stands to reason," Jaske said, "that we are going back home, so we are much nearer to that. It's just logic."

Mimmi looked around her allies now with triumph. "Tell that to Helve."

Jaske pushed Mimmi aside — it was all she could do — and took the nearest bunk. She sat up on it and tucked her knees under her chin.

She had lost.

And in a way it was fair enough. She had led these women into this. She had taken them all on the research trip out to the Sápmi. She was the most senior. They were students and she was a graduate. They were in her care and she had failed them.

20

HALFWAY THROUGH THE VOYAGE, steps boomed to the bunkroom and the man outside, the one they called Orvik, shoved Helve back in the room. She lay curled up in a foetal ball for the rest of the voyage, turned away from them. No one complained she had a bunk to herself.

After what seemed an eternity underwater, and the feeling that she was submerged and could hear nothing, like slipping through a hole in the ice, Jaske felt the submarine ascend with a sickening lurch. Activity. Men stomped up and down the gangways and the engines roared. Something clanked against the hull and echoed.

They had arrived. Wherever it was.

The women listened, fearful, some of them praying quietly. A few, Jaske noticed, were staring with dead eyes now, no longer seeing anything. It was perhaps the easy way out, to shut down and leave one's body. Anyone normal would do that after what had happened to Helve.

The boots tramped to the door and they heaved it open. Orvik shouted, "Out, *fittetryne!*"

The women filed out, some of them holding onto each other and tripping in the narrow door so that Orvik cursed and shoved them hard.

Jaske waited for them all to leave, pulling Helve from her bunk, where she seemed glued. She rose and crept out, head down and Jaske burned with impotent rage at Orvik's leering face.

The scissors in her pocket. She could take them out right now and plunge them into his eye.

"What are you waiting for, *Sámi fitte?* Fucking move!"

She stuffed her fist in her jeans pocket and stumbled past him. He shoved her forward and she careened down the gangway, followed the girls up the ladders through the fin, where the gush of cold air snatched her breath away.

Blinded by white light, she stepped out, treading carefully on the hull and clambering to the jetty with the others. One of the women held her hand as she came to shore. She felt hard land and squinted about her.

A cold sea, gun grey. And to the shore, a vast white tundra.

She couldn't hide her smile.

It was the same jetty at Vayda-Guba from where they had first set off. The submarine had skirted the entire Norwegian coast and circled to the northernmost point across to the patch that was Russia.

The border with Norway was close, but that didn't matter: this was the Finnmárku.

This was Sámi land.

The men filed the women down the jetty, a furious wind off the Barents Sea freezing them through to their bones. A bus waited — the same bus that had brought them here — and a handful of people carriers.

The women filed onto the bus without being asked, quickly huddling together in the seats. A Russian driver waited for them to climb aboard. Once all the women were on, they brought the Englishman and dumped him in the aisle on his stretcher. The stretcher-bearers stood at the front and muttered surly complaints with the driver.

The driver roared off and Jaske tried to hear what they were saying over the diesel squeal of the engine. Something about how it had all gone to shit, how this prisoner had fucked it all up for everyone, and how Nepravda was going to feed him feet first into a threshing machine till he talked. *Nepravda,* they said, whispering the word, like he was someone who could hear them talking about him, and someone who would kill you for mentioning his name, even under your breath. Just like they'd whispered about Beria. There was always another one, higher up, who was worse.

As the bus rattled down a long road across a vast plain of frozen tundra, Jaske thought *this is home.* Even though it was on the Russian side of the border, it was Sámi land. The Russians thought they owned it, but it was too remote and inhospitable to fully claim. There were isolated settlements, mostly military or research, many abandoned. Some of them even had names, unlike the roads. But the Russians didn't have the persistence for this landscape that the Sámi had. The Sámi belonged here and the Russians didn't.

The white plain ahead broke and the shadow of a settlement cracked the sheet of white.

She knew it.

This was where they'd first taken them. A remote abandoned military outpost. Nothing but a cluster of crumbling concrete blocks and a perimeter fence. Sometime in the Cold War, the Russians had thought this was a place worth laying down a marker. Planting a flag. They thought that because they dug a hole in the snow and took a shit, that made it Mother Russia.

She gripped the pair of scissors in her pocket and kindled the burning desire to kill every last one of them.

The perimeter fence loomed, the gate and the concrete sentry block beside it. Two guards stepped out and unchained the gate.

The convoy sailed through.

The Englishman groaned at a bump in the road.

Jaske reached down and wiped a sweaty slick of hair from his forehead. This man could not help them. If anyone had to get them out of here, she had to do it herself.

The bus sailed through the gates. She looked behind and, through a blizzard haze, saw the guards chain it up again.

21

THEY HAD LANDED. SOMEWHERE cold. Somewhere colder than he'd ever been. Blackwood felt his face puckering in protest. He had to pretend to be weaker than he was. He knew that. He had sunk into a sort of trance, enough to revive himself, heal a little, and simulate a fever. He shut his body down and found a place inside himself. But also enough awareness of the outside world to take it in, be responsive to danger, be aware of his surroundings.

Through eyelashes he'd spied the dock and the great white open space as they'd dumped him on the bus. There must be a base close by, because of the crappy old LAZ bus and the UAZ Hunter jeeps waiting for them. Russian plates. In this hostile environment, they would have to be within a few miles.

The sub had taken twenty hours. So they had most likely cruised to the first available Russian landing point. This was disturbing. What were they planning? If they wanted their money so badly, why retreat so far? It meant they were seriously regrouping.

After a short drive, he was aware of a checkpoint, the clanking of a gate and the shouting of sentries.

The girl, Jaske, close by, on the seat above him. Nervous excitement. Something in her that was different. The other girls all looked typically Scandinavian. Jaske had piercing blue eyes just like them but her hair was darker, her skin a shade of olive and her cheekbones more pronounced. She wore jeans and snow boots just like them, but her blue tunic, with its flash of red and green decorative collar, looked native.

There was something else about her that was different. She had hope.

The bus pulled to a stop and Blackwood allowed his consciousness to come to the surface, while still keeping his eyes half-closed. The stretcher-bearers tramped up the aisle, one of them stepping over Blackwood. They picked up the stretcher poles and humped him awkwardly down the steps. He nearly fell out into the snow, but they righted themselves, the one behind almost falling down the steps.

A vast white blur broken by a few brown concrete blocks. The men from the submarine stepped out of the Hunters. Someone barking orders on the bus. The women filed out and stood in the snow.

Beria prowled, standing close by. He took a look at Blackwood, grabbed his jaw and moved his head side to side. Blackwood moaned in fever.

Footsteps tramped through snow towards them.

One of the stretcher bearers said, "Fuck. Nepravda."

Fear among them. Even in Beria. It radiated off them.

Blackwood let his head loll to one side so he could see.

Beria took a deep breath and gritted his teeth. He stepped forward to meet the blur of a man marching towards them.

"Here," Beria said in English. "Here's your fucking patsy. Now tell me what the fuck happened."

The figure ignored Beria, stepped past him, and loomed close, crouching down to get a good look. A wry smile on a craggy face. A bushy beard flecked with grey.

"Jesus, Blackwood. Look at the state of you."

Blackwood blinked and tried to focus. Cold blue eyes, amused, sardonic.

No. It couldn't be. How the fuck?

It was *Curtis.*

"Take him away. Get him patched up. I need to question him."

The stretcher-bearers bundled on, breaking into a trot, eager to get away.

Blackwood felt himself passing out for real. He gripped the rod of the stretcher and braced himself against the jolting agony, screwing his eyes shut to the white glare as they bundled towards a concrete barrack with barred windows.

22

THROUGH HALF-CLOSED EYES, BLACKWOOD checked that they ran through a bunk room, much like the wooden hut on the previous island. There were beds laid out and unmade. This must have been where the women had stayed prior to being moved to the island. The men carrying him tramped through to a small room in the back and emptied him onto a single bed. It was a cell more than a room. A steel door with a grille.

One of the Norwegians came in with a bag and emptied out the medical supplies and set up a drip.

"Here you are, Shitboot," he sneered. "Get nice and better so you can feel the torture."

Blackwood moaned as if responding from a deep coma.

The man leaned in close. "All you fucking soldiers in it together like a gang of bumboys. You all so tough, but look at you: Rongstad, Pretke, Khryushka — all the soldiers are dead. Soon you will be dead too."

The man marched out to the bunk room. The sound of the women being herded in there. He came back and shoved Jaske in with him.

"Help this fucking ham rider."

He marched out and slammed the steel door but didn't lock it.

Jaske went to the barred window and peered out on tiptoes.

Blackwood tried to talk, words drying in his throat. She turned and looked surprised to see him awake. He pointed across the cell to the table and the medical supplies.

She came to him. "What?"

"Morphine," he croaked.

She nodded grimly and went to get it. There was a sink in the corner of the room and she filled a metal beaker and brought it to him.

Ice cold water that burned his temples. He slipped a morphine tablet into his mouth and swallowed.

She offered another.

He shook his head. "Not too much. Just one every five hours."

She frowned, not understanding.

He would last longer than five hours if he could. It needed to be a relief from the pain just enough so he could concentrate on reviving, and not have his energy sapped by struggling against pain. Not too much to zone him out totally. He needed to be active. Soon.

"Are we..." — he nodded towards the window — "where you said?"

She nodded.

"How close?" he asked. "To home. Your home?"

"Three hours, maybe. Driving. Two hours to the border, but another hour or more to the nearest Norwegian town. Only there are we safe."

Blackwood groaned and slumped back, gazing at the cracked ceiling. A four-hour drive to the border, no doubt along icy roads. In that bus — if he could steal it. Or get one of the Hunters and come back for the women. No, they would take them away. And Norwegian police wouldn't venture into Russia to storm a military base. It had to be all the women in the bus or nothing.

She seemed to read his thoughts. "You think we can't do it?"

"I could get us out of here," he said. "But those two hours to the border..."

"You can do it."

"How do you know?"

"We were doomed to be trafficked, till you showed up, and now we're almost home again. I believe you were sent here to free us."

She went to go but he reached out and pulled her wrist. Weaker than he thought.

"Don't let anyone know," he said. "I need them to think I'm no danger."

"And *are* you a danger?"

"Not yet."

She glanced at the steel door. The women talking low next door. "What is it they want to know?"

Could he trust her? It would be the easiest thing in the world to place a girl with him, get her to nurse him to health, all the time taking in any info he let slip. Trust was easier than interrogation. He could tell her that it wasn't just about the money; that Curtis all the way out here meant something else: something to do with Clocktower, something to do with one of those old operations.

"They just want to know where the money is," he said.

She nodded and walked through to the next room.

23

Beria said, "We just need to find out where the money is."

Curtis tramped along the icy path along the row of pens, a pace ahead, like he was a commander or something.

The sable jumped and flashed around in their chicken-wire cages, cartwheeling, railing against their confinement and Beria wondered idly for the thousandth time if they sensed the blood of their brothers or if it was simply their need to keep moving to stay warm. Active in the wild meant active in the cage.

These sable just didn't know they would never be free again.

There once was a time that wild sable was the most highly prized fur on the planet and farmed sable like this was less prized. But that didn't matter anymore. The wives of millionaires didn't know the difference, nor care.

Beria's men rolled out trolleys piled high with *sorocheks* — bundles of forty pelts. Others passed with plastic storage boxes full of hacked off sable legs, all furry and bloody.

Curtis halted and checked the men as they passed, like he was mentally totting up the profit. "We'll get it out of Blackwood," he said. "I'll see to it personally."

Beria nodded. There was something else, something Curtis wasn't saying, as if another game was being played entirely and this whole botched operation involving ten million pounds was just a small part of it.

Beria barked out orders to the men, even though they knew what they were doing and needed no instruction. To remind myself, he thought. To remind myself I'm the commander of this military outpost, not this English mercenary.

He spat on the snow to get rid of the bitter taste in his mouth.

They turned at the drone of an engine. Two vehicles coming through the gate, waved through by the sentries. VW Transporter Syncros, unmarked, black.

"Here's Den Bla Vesken," Beria said.

Curtis said nothing.

Of course it was Bla Vesken. It could be no one else. Beria cursed himself and spat again. Curtis and his psychopathic silence made you want to fill the air with inanities. Here was The Blue Bag. Their Norwegian smuggling contact. The codename to be used at all times to maintain his anonymity. No one needed to say it because everyone knew it. That was why his men were unloading the *sorocheks*.

The vehicles churned snow as they pulled up. None of the men got out. Bla Vesken was giving out last orders. As if they hadn't had time for that on the three-hour drive across the border, down those not-so-secret paths that weren't frozen over and left unguarded by border patrol.

Curtis stood silent and stared, revealing nothing. A snowman with pebble eyes.

Bla Vesken and one of his men jumped out of the first vehicle, and two in the second vehicle followed. His three men began loading their transporters with the *sorochek* bundles, the crates of bloody sable legs and boxes of vodka, chinking as they humped them into the cars.

Bla Vesken left them to do the grunt work and trudged over to greet Curtis and Beria, panting for breath, overweight and out of shape. An amateur.

When he got within five yards, his smile dropped, like he could read it in their faces that the mission had gone to shit.

"There's no money," said Curtis.

"No money? What happened?"

"The deal didn't happen. There were complications."

Bla Vesken looked from one to the other, trying to read their cold faces, hoping they would laugh and reveal it was all a joke. "I gave you those girls."

"The sale hasn't been made," said Beria, shrugging, as if it were nothing to do with him. Ten fucking million pounds.

"You were supposed to make that deal," Bla Vesken said, puffing out his chest, like a husband prodded by his bitch of a wife to complain to a restaurant manager. "I supplied the product. I held up my end of the deal. You can't make the sale? That's your problem."

"I wouldn't lecture me on what is and isn't my problem," said Beria. "Not while you sit on this side of the border."

"Border?" Bla Vesken waved his arm to indicate the vast dark void beyond the compound. "With two metres of snow on the ground there *is* no border."

"We could always end our arrangement right this second."

Bla Vesken's mouth fell open a little.

Beria took out his Makarov and Bla Vesken cringed. Beria slid back the chamber and popped out the round. He slapped the bullet into the fat man's gloved hand. "Would this be payment enough, or would you need the entire magazine?"

Bla Vesken coloured, anger flaring in his cheeks. He stepped back. "There's no need for that," he wheedled. "We do business. We've done business for years. You Russians sit out here in your shitty military camp, selling surplus military equipment, cheap vodka, running your illegal sable farm, selling everything that isn't bolted down, and we take it off your hands and give you good money for it. Good Western money. Dollars, not shitty roubles."

Bla Vesken wheeled and walked away, pacing in the snow.

Curtis watched him, as if all this was beneath him. As if this was two children squabbling over who gets to go on the bike. It was annoying as fuck.

"And you come to me with your heroin deal and yes, I'm grateful for that, but it's me who suggests adding the women to the deal. It's me who gives you the intel on where twenty young women can be found. I do all that and now you fuck it up and tell me I don't get my money. Just remember who it is that eases the way for you, sees that it all goes smoothly across the border."

Beria thought of the submarine and was about to tell Bla Vesken they didn't need access over the shitty border anymore; they could sail it right around Norway and land anywhere else who would take their business.

But they'd done that, and BBC World News were reporting a burning farmhouse on the Scottish coast and fifty or more dead bodies. It was a clusterfuck. A daisy cutter bomb on a school.

For now, this small-time amateur crook who thought he was a big commissar would have to do.

He was about to tell him all that, but Curtis spoke.

"We have the money."

Bla Vesken stopped pacing and looked from Curtis to Beria and back again. "What do you mean?"

"We have your money," said Curtis wearily. "But not right now. We'll have it all tomorrow. Will you allow me twenty-four hours to secure it?"

Bla Vesken looked unsure. Beria wondered what game Curtis was playing now. There was no money.

"I would appreciate it," Curtis said.

"Twenty-four hours, you say?"

"You have my word," said Curtis.

Bla Vesken glanced back at his men clustered around their Transporter Syncros. He nodded. "Are you sure you haven't made the deal and now you're just cutting me out of my share? I mean, how do I know?"

"You can come and see the product," Curtis said, indicating the bunker, twenty yards away.

"The product?"

"The girls. They're here."

"They're *here?*"

"Yes," said Beria, "we had to bring them back, of course."

"Jesus fucking Christ. What if they see me? They could recognize me and my men."

"I suppose they could," said Curtis. "That would be very bad for you. Even once we sell them on, they would still, one day, get the word out about who arranged their kidnapping."

"Why didn't you tell me you'd brought them back here?"

"You didn't ask," Curtis said.

"Fucking hell. I'm out of here. We come back tomorrow and you'd better have that money."

Bla Vesken scrambled back to his men and in a moment, they were slamming doors and driving off full pelt for the gate.

Beria watched the two Transporter Syncros waved through the gate and beyond till the red taillights faded to nothing in the blackness. "Why did you tell him you'd have the money for him tomorrow?"

"So I didn't have to shoot him right here and now."

The Englishman marched off to the control bunker and Beria wondered if perhaps 'Nepravda' had a conscience after all. But then he called back over his shoulder, "Bring the prisoner to the interrogation room. It's time."

24

BLACKWOOD WOKE FROM A soothing fug of morphine blankness. Rough hands dragged him off the bunk. Someone slapped him awake. The stench of vodka breath. Two Russian soldiers.

The abusive Norwegian looked on with a malicious grin and said, "Time for your interrogation, Shitboot."

The Russians strapped him into a wheelchair and rolled him through the bunk room next door. Blackwood, through slitted eyes, took in the women huddled on their bunks with the spectral, dazed stares of bomb survivors. He'd seen that look before. It was always on women. Bosnia. Sierra Leone. Kabul.

And his daughter.

They wheeled him out through the door and a blast of frigid air burned his lungs. The white glare of the tundra void blinded him, but he blinked it away to take in the surroundings. Concrete blocks. At least ten of them. The old LAZ bus that had brought them here sheltered in an open carport building made of three containing concrete walls and a corrugated tin roof. Five UAZ Hunter jeeps parked up. Unmanned. That sentry post out by the gate: only a couple of armed guards out there.

They trundled past a concrete barrack. Men's voices inside, shouting, playing. A card game or something. Music. Drinking. There weren't many more men than had come here from the island. Maybe this wasn't a military base. Maybe it had only been Curtis and those sentries and the drivers who'd been here waiting for them to come back. That put the enemy forces at about twenty heads.

A row of cages. Sable squeaking, scampering, somersaulting.

They wheeled him to a smaller block and bundled through heavy doors out of the howling wind to welcome silence. They wheeled him through to a shabby office that looked like it had been forgotten twenty years ago. Blackwood slumped his head forward, to look like he was more fucked up than he really was.

They stopped and one of them yanked his head back. His eyes rolled open and he looked into the grinning face of Curtis.

"You look better."

Blackwood felt drool slide down his chin. It was important to not let it show in his eyes. Glaze them over, like the women in the bunks — replicate the dazed, dead eyes of the bomb survivor, catatonic — or this man would read it and detect he was stalling.

"So what happened at that farmhouse?"

"Farmhouse?" Blackwood mumbled. Too much.

A sharp slap across his face cut through the morphine haze like a scalpel. Something cracked in his neck.

One of the Russian soldiers. The next would be a punch.

Blackwood lowed a bovine moan.

"In fact, I know what happened. It's all over the news. What I want to know is, where's the money?"

"Burned."

"If it's burned, I don't need you," Curtis leered. A threat. "Where is it?"

"Gone."

Another stinging crack across the face. *Gone*, he thought. *Gone. Gone. Gone.* Get your strength back but pretend to be weaker than you are.

"You know, Blackwood, it doesn't really surprise me that this operation turned into a bloodbath only days after you were released from prison. I almost expected it."

A sharp look from the other Russian in the room. Beria. The one who'd captured him at the jetty. The smartest of them. The one who'd anticipated the opposite.

Blackwood shrugged and grunted. It would be so easy to sink back into sleep, but his mind raced. how to convince these people that he was weaker than he was, maybe even close to death, but that he still had information.

Curtis leapt up and took a fistful of Blackwood's hair. "Look at you. Look at what you are now. All because you wouldn't kill a reporter."

Through the fog of memory. So much shit had gone down since then. Some journalist who'd asked the wrong questions. Blackwood glared right back at Curtis. "He wasn't really an enemy of the state, though, was he?"

"Your job wasn't to make that call." Curtis shoved him free and wheeled round. Pacing now, hands behind his back. "Is it any wonder Britain went to the dogs if even the death squad soldiers like you were questioning everything?"

"I didn't think..." — Blackwood faked a cough — "...protecting some politician who got his dick caught in a boy's arse was really a matter of national security."

"But you didn't just refuse to kill the reporter. You gave him a file on Clocktower. The whole operation. Feeding some commie reporter our state secrets."

"Says the British agent who's working with the Russians."

"Russia isn't communist anymore, Blackwood. Where have you been?"

"I *have* been out of the loop, I'll admit."

"But you never change the regime, really. You just put a different badge on the old gangsters. Wave a new flag. It's always the same people. They can switch from communist to fascist in the blink of an eye — whatever keeps them in power."

Beria hissed but said nothing.

Curtis ignored him. "It's the same the world over. Even in your precious British democracy. An elite gang carving it all up between them and going through the pantomime of democracy — staging it for the proles. Anyone who really believes in that democracy shit has to be dealt with."

"That's what Clocktower was about?"

"Of course it was, Blackwood."

"I thought it was about protecting our country... eliminating... enemies?"

"It was."

"We didn't kill terrorists," Blackwood spluttered. "We murdered journalists who asked questions... politicians who demanded enquiries... whistleblowers."

"Not all enemies are foreign. They don't all parachute in wearing uniforms and carrying weapons."

"And what are you doing out here? You some kind of kingmaker now?"

Curtis stopped pacing and grinned his smug grin. "I'm not a politician, Blackwood. I have much more power than that."

Blackwood coughed, wheezed and slumped, like that outburst had half killed him. Stupid. He'd revealed he was fitter than he was letting on.

Curtis came closer. "Now, enough of this *Question Time* bullshit. Let's discuss the location of ten million pounds, shall we?"

He dug his fist into Blackwood's gaping wound. Like a knife into his guts.

Blackwood let out a sharp squeal of animal pain. Like those sable in their cages. Louder than he wanted. Did it betray he was not as fucked up as he pretended? He didn't care. There was no way to stop that. If it wasn't for the morphine, it might have been louder and peppered with obscenities and everything he knew about the money. Every little detail they wanted to know just to end that pain.

He wondered if he would sell out his own daughter to them. Give her up. Just to end the pain.

Gone, gone, gone.

25

DECEMBER 9TH, 2004. CREDENHILL, Hereford.

Curtis's office was poky, functional, the only ornamentation a bottle of whisky on the filing cabinet behind him. Lagavulin.

Blackwood had copied him. A fresh recruit straight into Sierra Leone. This commanding officer who didn't neck beer like other officers did. Like Colonel Curtis, Blackwood had sipped at a single malt in the mess, insisted on a decent single malt wherever in the world they happened to be. Blackwood had copied him because it had seemed particular. Refined. The action of a sophisticated, intelligent soldier, not some bayonet.

Tony Blair's portrait smiled down at them. A smug smile. The smile of a smug wanker you couldn't trust.

"If it's about what happened in Basra, sir—"

"At ease, Blackwood." Curtis indicated the seat.

Blackwood sat and tried to relax. Too tense. This was a reprimand.

"Your report recommends you for a certain type of work," Curtis said.

"I don't understand, sir."

"Your psyche report," said Curtis. "And, of course, my own observations of you in the field."

What was this? Some kind of psychiatric evaluation. Were they saying he was a psycho or something?

"Don't be offended." Curtis smiled, gently amused. His grey flint eyes betraying something — an understanding. A recognition. You and I are just alike.

"I'm not offended, sir. It's just—"

"Your report suggests you have an aptitude for this kind of work. You're efficient, follow orders to the letter, but you also have an ability for improvisation. You think on your feet, adapt to extreme situations."

I do the opposite, Blackwood thought. It had been something he'd tried to suppress. A reflex that might not suit the military. But it had got him out of the fire more than once. Maybe this was what they meant. Not that he had killed without letting it bother him. No post-traumatic stress. No guilt. He'd done the job and never thought about it again. But that when he was in a hole, he did the opposite of his training, his instincts. He did the unexpected.

"You've served continuously for six years. Sierra Leone, Afghanistan, Iraq. I suppose you're itching to get back into it?"

"I'm sitting on my hands a bit, sir."

"Well, I've got something for you."

Blackwood felt the sigh of relief explode inside him. He held it in, to give nothing away, but Curtis smiled again. He saw everything.

"Afghanistan is in the hands of the Black Rats now. It's all just seeing out an occupation, training the Iraqis to avoid suicide bombers. Routine stuff. We've got other work to do."

Blackwood sat up an inch taller in the chair and leaned forward.

"What we do is off the books."

"Off the books, sir?"

"There are no campaign medals for what we do. Our country needs someone assassinated, we do it."

"Assassinated?"

"Black ops. Call it what you like. Clocktower allows our government to get to dangerous people we can't touch by normal means."

"Why can't we touch them, sir?"

"Good question. I don't mind you asking it. The problem is, in a modern democracy, a war can be hampered. We're fighting with one hand tied behind our back. It's not like in the Second World War when the whole nation was behind it, everyone doing their bit. Most modern wars have to be secret. The public don't want them. The politicians are scared. The media focus on dead children and dolls in the rubble. They want their cosy, privileged lives but they don't want the wars that guarantee it. So sometimes we have to fight for democracy in secret."

Curtis sat back and read his face.

Blackwood nodded. He'd heard the rumours. All kinds of off-the-books assassination units in the seventies. Older buddies had talked in hushed tones of the 'Feathermen': ex-SAS guys, a black ops unit killing people the government couldn't touch by other means.

"How do you feel about that?"

Blackwood shrugged. "Isn't it the same as killing an enemy combatant in the field?"

"Some would argue not."

"A sniper can take someone out from a mile away and the poor bastard never sees it coming. Everyone's okay with that. Or we drop bombs on a city."

"You think there's a difference?" Curtis asked, amused.

"Seems to me something like that might be more... surgical. Precise."

Curtis nodded. "Very good. Welcome to Clocktower." He rose. The meeting was over.

Blackwood got up. "Thank you, sir."

"Briefing in Hut 13 at 0800 tomorrow."

Blackwood walked out to cold winter air and looked up at the clocktower that stood sentinel over Credenhill. Hereford. He'd always thought he was part of this, but now it seemed he was in some invisible part of this.

26

THEY SLAPPED HIM AWAKE. Blackwood didn't know how long he'd been out in that comfortable morphine haze, but it was cold and his body ached in many places it hadn't ached before.

It was the psycho called Orvik. "Wake up, Shitboot!" he screamed.

The light so harsh it slammed his eyeballs, He tried to cover his face but Orvik slapped his feeble hands away.

Curtis and Beria waiting with grim smiles. Two Russian guards behind them. They were going to torture him again. He knew he couldn't stand it this time. He didn't have any strength left in him.

Curtis smiled sympathetically. Strolled around a desk and took a seat. He poured two glasses of whisky and offered one to Blackwood.

The glass, winking amber gold, was a million miles away. Someone put it in his cold, dead hand and raised it to his mouth. He tasted floral grassy menthol freshness. A spring day in a field, somewhere beautiful, somewhere you'd long to be. Not like this place. This barren, freezing shithole of a place at the end of the world.

This was like that time before. Sitting across from Curtis. The officer making him an offer over a dram. Drawing him into his web of lies. The only thing missing was the portraits of the queen and the Prime Minister on the wall behind him. On this wall it was Putin.

"You know how hard it is to get a decent Scotch out here, Blackwood?"

"Easier at home. You should try it."

The words came from him, from his slack mouth, as if someone else was saying them, someone who could think straight.

"It's a rare treat, to share a good Scotch with someone who appreciates it. Not that vodka shit."

He was aware of the Russians bristling with offence. They were also a million miles away and not in the room at all. Blackwood tried not to laugh, but it was so hard not to when you felt such a profound sense of ease with the world. He was flying, floating, grinning.

"Where are we?" he said. "Above the Arctic Circle?"

"Good guess."

"Not really, by the way my balls are freezing off."

"Murmansk region. An area they call the Finnmark."

"Lapland? And you're Father Christmas?"

"I've never been what you thought," Curtis said, smiling, taking a sip of whisky, savouring it.

"Been looking at the place," Blackwood said, aware he was slurring his words.

"If I'd known you were coming, I'd have tidied."

"Former military outpost, yes?"

"What makes you think it still isn't?"

"Looks more like a criminal operation now. A mafia bolthole."

Curtis grinned. "You know, with all this chaos recently, it's difficult to tell the difference."

"You sound delighted at that."

"I do take pride in it."

He was talking as if he was responsible. As if he'd brought it into being. How much influence did he have out here?

"Isn't this where we planted those surveillance dishes?"

Curtis flinched and glanced at Beria. It was a microscopic gesture, but Blackwood saw it like he'd jumped back and screamed, *Not in front of the Russian!*

Beria gave a slight smile. The indulgent smile of a former enemy now an ally, letting bygones be bygones, or the smug glower of the spy who knew all about it.

"Microwave comms," said Blackwood. "Isn't this where we planted those microwave receivers in the 80s?"

Blackwood had been told the story. Curtis had rambled about it more than once. The Russian microwave tech had a weakness in the system. If you stood halfway between two towers with a microwave receiver, you could hear every word. They were clocking the traffic between Moscow and Murmansk. You'd get a logistics list for the day and know which subs had just returned from patrol, what their status was, how long they'd be in dock, what spares they needed, the readiness status of all the fighter squadrons at the air base.

Beria looked less indulgent now. His cheek twitching. Russian military really hated having their incompetence pointed out to them.

"You think you know a lot," Curtis said.

"I know you're a traitor."

Curtis laughed. "Oh. Blackwood, you don't even know what war you're fighting, who's who, what the sides are."

"I know you've switched to the Russians."

"The Cold War was over years ago, Blackwood."

"Yeah, and we won."

"Ha. You thought you won. And for a while, it really looked like it. But you thought a Cold War with communist Russia was dangerous? Try it with the mad fuckers who are running the show now."

"You used to be a soldier, Curtis," Blackwood spat.

"So did you, Blackwood. Then you became a criminal too. Isn't it funny how that happens? Tell me, how did you get involved in crime?"

A shadow falling over him. Bad memory. A cataclysm of bad luck. Working a door at a shitty nightclub in London, to earn a bit of extra money off the books. A troublemaker he had to beat up. Arrest. Dishonourable discharge. The nightclub owner taking him on as hired muscle. From soldier to criminal gang member in a few shitty days.

"Accident," Blackwood said.

Curtis smirked. "There are no accidents, Blackwood. You'll see that in time."

What did he mean? The smug smirk that said *I know more than you know,* and the implied threat that there was more of this *I know more than you* to come.

"You think I'm impressed?" Blackwood laughed. "Look at you, just some washed up vet reduced to wanking for coins from the enemy. They're laughing at you, Curtis. Look at what you are now."

"Enough of this shit," Curtis said. He flicked his fingers and, like an obedient dog, the stooge called Orvik ran at Blackwood and punched him in the gut.

Blackwood laughed long and hard. Maybe. He wasn't sure if the laughter was inside him or echoing off the walls. Or if it was coming from everyone else around him, Maybe they were all laughing at him.

Curtis's face loomed in close. So close Blackwood could smell the whisky on his breath.

"You have no idea what I've wrought. We've already won the war, and you didn't even know it was happening. You retweeted our bullets and committed mass suicide. The most docile army in the world, submitting quietly to euthanasia. Pulling the plug on their own life support because we told them to. That's what I've done. You don't even *know.*"

He was rambling. But he was right: Blackwood didn't know what the hell he was talking about. The insane ramblings of a rogue general in the jungle, gone mad on a diet of tree bark, bullfrogs and native worship, thinking himself a God. This was what happened when assassins thought they were kingmakers; this was what happened when the hatchet thought it was the sceptre.

A bolt of insufferable electric pain shot right through his soul and he shuddered to keep himself from leaving his body.

His daughter. He'd saved her. She had the money. She was driving away in the car. He knew the car's registration number and everything. He knew she was meeting her mother, somewhere between that farmhouse in Scotland and the long dead road to London. Manchester, he'd suggested, but wherever it happened.

He wondered if he was thinking all of this or saying it aloud.

Perhaps the key was to not think about it.

He hid them in the deepest, most secret corner of his mind. He locked his daughter and her mother, and the haul of money, in the cellar. But the house was burning down and he couldn't be sure he hadn't called out to them through the flames.

Curtis and his private army were stomping down the steps and banging at the cellar door.

The thing was, once you lost your mind, all your dirty secrets just came tumbling out.

Perhaps, without even knowing it, he'd given them away.

27

January 8th, 2005. Hereford.

Blackwood slumped into the worn leather of the booth, the wood beneath creaking in protest. The Clocktower group, his new brothers-in-arms, filled the spaces around him. The air was thick with the musk of sweat and ale as glasses clinked, frothy heads of beer sloshing over the rims with each toast and cheer.

"Here's to not dying!" someone bellowed, a sentiment echoed by raucous laughter.

The pub, a fixture in Hereford and no stranger to military patronage, hummed with their presence.

Curtis raised his pint glass, his voice slicing through the din. "To us, the unseen hand!"

"Unseen hand!" they roared.

Blackwood tipped back his pint and locked eyes with Curtis, a silent understanding passing between them.

The celebration swelled around them, a cocoon of camaraderie and shared purpose. But even as he joined in, Blackwood checked the pub for threats, vigilant, watchful.

Across the bar, locals threw looks of unspoken animosity. He shrugged it off. Old stories of bruised egos and broken bones had taught them to tolerate these squaddies that invaded their bars.

Curtis sank his pint of beer like the men, not sipping at a single malt like he usually did.

As pint followed pint, the air thickened with laughter and then a yelling chorus of *I Don't Want to Join the Army*, all screaming with relish every *fuck* and *bollocks*.

Five pints in, Blackwood leaned back, his head swimming, and listened, half-amused, half-disgusted, as the talk turned to tours past: of Iraq, Sierra Leone and Northern Ireland, of ragheads, jungle bunnies and Fenians.

His stomach churned at the crassness. A familiar discomfort, the kind that came with the territory of testosterone-fuelled bravado. He sipped his beer more slowly, bitterness on his tongue.

"Another for the brotherhood!" Curtis called out, his voice losing its edge to the booze, yet still commanding, still impossible to ignore.

The room swayed. Laughter and slurred toasts collided with the clink of empty pint glasses. Curtis ordered whisky at last. But not a dram. The whole bottle.

Blackwood squinted as the amber liquid was poured. It filled twelve glasses lined up like soldiers on parade. The scent hit him first — earthy, pungent, a hint of disinfectant.

"Drink up, lads," Curtis ordered.

"Christ, it smells like fucking hospital floors!"

"What is it? Fucking brake fluid?"

Faces contorted. Curses spat. One soldier bolted for the door, hand clamped over his mouth.

Curtis raised his own glass, eyes twinkling with mirth or madness. "This is the good stuff, boys."

His lips met the rim again, a slow sip savoured. The others watched, some trying to mimic his appreciation and failing.

Blackwood sipped, almost a breath, and the liquid morphed on his tongue. It seared, mellowed, then bloomed. Cleaning fluid at first, then a swerve to savoury roast beef, then sweet roasted plums. Three courses in one gulp.

His comrades laughed loud over the table cluttered with empty glasses and half-filled pints. His eyes landed on a nearly drained pint, froth clinging to the side. With a covert glance, he switched his full pint with the orphaned one. No one noticed. Another swig, the beer now bland after to the whisky's complexity. Eighth or ninth pint? Numbers blurred together, indistinct as the faces around him.

"Off the books," filtered through the din, pulling Blackwood back from the brink of nausea. "Dirty secrets," followed, tethering him to Curtis's unravelling monologue.

Curtis leaned forward, the Scotch bottle clutched like a sceptre. "Borders," he spat, the word heavy with disdain. "We're here to keep the borders in place. But what about Norway? Fucking Russia?"

Others laughed, like Curtis had made a joke.

"Concrete posts? The permafrost spits them out like fucking toothpicks," Curtis muttered, eyes glazed, peering into nothing, lost in memories or madness.

Blackwood steadied himself against the table as the room took a slow, dizzying turn. He focused on Curtis, the man's voice cutting through the pub's haze.

"You fucking watch out," he slurred. "Top brass will screw you over. Never to trust your commanding officer."

"Even you?" Blackwood's voice cut through the laughter around them.

Curtis locked eyes with Blackwood. Venom flickered there, then faded into a sloppy grin. "Especially me."

Bodies swayed and stumbled. One soldier lurched toward the door, another doubled over, retching. Their descent into inebriation was methodical, almost ritualistic. They peeled away from the group one by one — some to the bogs, some outside to take the night air like a cold shower. At least one of them staggered off back to barracks, like his homing beacon had set off.

Blackwood's world pitched and yawed. He focused on Curtis, trying to find an anchor in the captain's words.

The old soldier's gaze had turned glassy, his attention fixed on the bottle cradled in his hands. "Fucking Linhammar," he muttered, pouring another drink. "Every time, they shoot you down like Linhammar."

The name hung in the air, heavy and foreboding.

"What's Linhammar?"

Time warped, stretched thin and snapped back. Curtis, a statue in the chaos, took an age to respond. It was a moment dragged over months, the tick of the pub's old clock stretching into eternity.

"No one knows," Curtis finally said, his voice a low rumble. "One day the whole world will know about it."

Blackwood nodded, but the room spun on, a carousel of muffled sounds and blurred faces. At some point the darkness took him and he woke startled in his bunk.

28

THEY DUMPED HIM IN a wheelchair and carted him off.
The chair creaked through a drab office block. A harsh
blast of freezing wind iced the thread of drool down his
chin as they went over to the block where the girls were
kept.

Through a slit in his bruised eye he noticed there
were two men stationed on the door inside, but no one
outside. Because no one would attack out here. Their
eyes were only concentrated on the threat from inside
the bunk room — from the girls, and from this prisoner.

And then he couldn't think why he needed to know
that.

They pushed him through the bunk room and the
women fell silent as the dead man trundled through.

That was right, he was dead and this was his funeral.
Russian pallbearers carrying him to his bed, his grave.

The Norwegian cackled and shouted for Jaske. "You, *Sámi fitte!* See to Shitboot here. Make him better for the next round."

There must be some mistake. There would be no next round, he was dead.

But if there was a next round of torture, that meant he'd given nothing away.

They wheeled him into the back room and emptied him out. Blackwood hit the floorboards and slammed down like a sack of rubbish and didn't move. It wasn't pretence. He couldn't move. Just wanted to stay still and lie like this for the rest of his life.

Jaske's boots clattered on the floorboards and resonated through his forehead.

Blackwood wondered why this Norwegian guard spoke English. To him, yes, so he could deliver his insults more effectively, but why speak English to Jaske, too? Perhaps it was all a performance for Blackwood's benefit.

He just didn't know yet if Jaske was in on the performance.

His eyes closed and he fell into the comforting void of his grave.

29

BERIA STOMPED ALONG THE row of cages, the sable turning and rattling as he passed, squealing their terror.

He was muttering to himself and pressed his lips shut tight. Not against the cold but because he was muttering to himself, sub-vocalising, like a crazy person, a person with no self-control.

But he had no control. Not here. Not with Curtis here. Beria was the commander-in-chief of this operation. Beria could order his own men around and do whatever he wanted. But Curtis was in charge of the criminal enterprise with those inept Norwegians.

Once again, it gnawed at his soul that Moscow had intervened in this. The whole point of the criminal operations here — the sable farm, the vodka, the smuggling of everything that wasn't bolted to the floor — was that Moscow didn't have to know. But it turned out they had known all the time and didn't care. Only now had they sent this mercenary to commandeer everything.

What angered him wasn't that he had been discovered in his petty criminal activity, so much as they had promoted a foreigner to take it over.

As he entered Curtis's bunker, he cursed himself for not bringing a personal guard. Three, no four, good officers to outnumber Curtis's two. Coming alone like this only made it more apparent that he was the underling being summoned to a superior.

Inside, Curtis was at his desk, a glass of golden whisky before him. That vile stuff he sipped at for hours like a woman instead of knocking back in one manly shot. His two guards stood to attention behind him, to be intimidating. The Norwegian criminal, Orvik, stood before him, his head bowed in shame. The only member of the Norwegian criminal gang left now. They had all been killed.

Beria slumped in a leather armchair, swept his ushanka off his head and said, "What is it now?"

"This idiot," Curtis said.

"You told us to do it," Orvik spluttered. "Get him better, you said."

"And it didn't occur to you that us torturing him might not work if you were still giving him morphine?"

"Morphine?" Beria hissed, aghast. He rubbed his face, wishing he could rub away this fresh catastrophe. It was one fuck up after another.

"I just did what you told me to do!" Orvik yelled.

There was something about his defiance that had Beria reaching for his pistol. It was the demeanour of a criminal, not a soldier. One who thought he could shout at a superior. This was what happened when you invited criminals onto a barracks.

"Fucking imbeciles," Beria hissed, digging out his pack of Winston cigarettes. He lit one and sucked in bitter nicotine, again not asking permission. Fuck Curtis and fuck his criminal gang and fuck Moscow too.

Curtis stood and turned to his personal guard, taking them to one side, the three of them muttering in the corner of the room.

Orvik looked around in wild panic. The stupid Norwegian *blatnoy* thought they were arranging a firing squad. It was not so stupid an idea. Beria would happily take out his pistol right here and paint the wall with his brains, but, to his intense annoyance, it was Curtis's call.

Beria seethed over his cigarette. Curtis's personal guard were two Russian soldiers who were close to Curtis and Curtis alone. They had come with him from Moscow.

It annoyed Beria that they could not be turned. He had tried numerous times to co-opt them into his confidence, to make them informers. He had thought it would be easy. But they remained steadfast to this interloping Englishman. As if their orders were from the President himself. They were an imperial guard, loyal to a foreign *nayomnitsa*. For some unfathomable reason, the President had given this man unrivalled power. It was a fucking insult to the Motherland.

Curtis finished whispering and his guards stomped out without saluting Beria, without acknowledging his existence.

"So what now?" Beria said. "Take him off the morphine."

"No," said Curtis. "Increase it. Double the dose."

"What?"

"Make him nice and mellow. He'll feel at peace with the world and very willing to talk. We do the opposite."

Orvik looked from one to the other, watching a game of tennis, his stupid *blatnoy* face all red, empurpled with rage. Where had he heard that phrase before? A joke about a commanding officer. Someone had made it. Someone way, way back in the past.

"You heard," Beria said. "Go fucking do it before I put a bullet through your stupid fucking skull."

Orvik stormed out.

Beria sprang up and stubbed his cigarette out on Curtis's rug, grinding it with his boot. He put his *ushanka* back on and said, "I guess we wait till he's nice and mellow again. Let me know when he's ready."

Curtis said nothing. Beria smirked as he left, but it froze on his lips as the howling blast of winter night assaulted him.

Curtis's guards crossed him on the path and said nothing, like he wasn't the commander of this station. They were carrying a metal suitcase, one of them holding it to his chest.

Beria paused and watched them go not to Curtis's bunker but veer off towards where the girls and Blackwood were held. What were they up to?

He crept after them, trying to make his boots not crump so loudly in the snow. The noise of chatter from the men's mess hut covered him.

Curtis's guards went to the carport and he heard them loading one of the UAZ Hunter jeeps.

He silently skirted the rear of the carport and listened.

"There."

"Be careful."

"It's not active."

"Still."

They clunked the door shut, one of the rear doors, and tramped off across the compound.

Beria stood still in the dark shadow of the carport and wondered, what could possibly be in the suitcase that was so important? And where was Curtis going with it?

He cursed himself. Why was he skulking around his own command post, like some fucking spy?

Beria spat and headed for his hut, blazing defiance against the cruel wind that swept in off the Barents Sea.

And for some reason he found himself thinking of his propaganda training at the academy. His professor had instructed them all on American and British war movies, and pointed out they were all about individual heroism, the cult of the individual. But our great Russian war movies — all those classics about the Great Patriotic War, emphasized a very different belief that was central to the Russian psyche. He scratched it on the blackboard in capital letters.

Victory At Any Cost.

Only Russia had this tenacity, this unwavering resolution for victory, no matter what the cost. There was no self-doubt, no relativism, no weighing up the morals of the situation. These ways of thinking were only encouraged in our enemies. But to Russia, only one thing mattered: victory.

Nothing, no belief, however sacred, would not be sacrificed for victory.

Beria had put up his hand. What about Russia itself? Our patriotism. Would that be sacrificed?

The professor had smiled, polished his glasses, mulling it over, then said, "Do you recall that when the Nazis invaded Russia, we were willing to set fire to half of the country to drive them back. Our country. We burned it to the ground rather than let them have it. Victory. At. Any. Cost."

It was all bullshit. And here was the proof. Our military outposts handed over to foreign mercenaries. No one gave a fuck about victory.

He trudged to his hut and the promise of vodka. He would obliterate this feeling. Perhaps send for one of the girls again. Maybe the same one he'd taken on the submarine. Or that Sámi girl. It would be more pleasurable to break her, she showed such defiance. Yes, she would be good sport. He was in the mood to destroy someone.

30

JASKE STAYED IN THE back room while Blackwood was gone. She no longer wanted to be around the other women, either scared or ashamed, she couldn't tell. There were no words anymore, nothing to say, only sullen resentment and comatose horror. This was as close to death as it was possible to be while still breathing. If they killed her now, it would be release.

But still she held onto that buzz of hope fluttering in her breast. This was Sámi land beneath them, no matter if it was called *Russia* on a map. This was her land. She was a few hours from home.

They dragged Blackwood's carcass back and dumped him on the bed. The two Russian sentries cursed and retreated, back through to the bunk room.

Orvik went to the door and she thought he was going to walk through but he kicked it shut and turned to her, rage blazing in his eyes.

What had she done now?

She glanced at Blackwood, lying prone on his bunk, dead to the world.

"You think that sack of rubbish will protect you?"

Orvik was on her in a moment. He yanked her by her hair and she yelped as he slammed her against the desk and turned her round. Sharp pain flared through her pelvis. Had the impact broken it?

He slammed her face down and growled, *"Sámifitte!"* He was all animal now.

Tugging at her jeans, yanking them down over her hips. He didn't unbutton or unzip, just the primal force of his fist tearing them over her hips, exposing her. Her hand reached to pull them back up.

He gripped her hair tighter and slammed her head on the desk.

She reeled, dazed.

Her fingers groping for her jeans. The pocket. The scissors.

He was fumbling at his own trousers, grunting and panting.

Her fingers found the pocket. She couldn't get into it. Bent over. She would break her finger the wrong way to reach into the pocket.

She twisted her arm around, right to the limit, till it burned, fingers probing inside the pocket, touching the warm steel. One finger found the loop. She pulled it out and the curve of the sharp point scraped her thigh.

"Fucking still," he grunted.

Scrambling, furious, urgent, like he couldn't find his dick, like someone had stolen it.

The scissors firm in her fist now, between her legs, hidden from him. She thought for a wild moment she would reach under herself and cut his balls off. But no, she couldn't reach that way.

She twisted, jerked around, and sent him off balance. And in a single instant she realized he had one hand on his cock, trying to make himself hard because he couldn't get it up.

Her arm arced around and she punched him in the neck.

A spurt of red. Her hand fell.

He stared, shocked, like she'd slapped him and he was going to punch her face in for it. The scissors stuck in his neck. Blood squirted.

He went to scream but choked on his own blood. A throttled gurgling. He was drowning.

His fingers fumbled at his belt, below his flaccid, sad little penis, trying to get his gun, but he was drowning.

She shoved him off her and he fell back and hit the floorboards with a crash. The blood was still spurting out of his neck, sending out a spray across the floor.

She sat back against the desk, pulling her jeans back up, staring at him, not knowing what to do.

He gripped the scissors, yanked them out and clamped a hand on his neck to stop the blood torrent. He raised his head, eyes burning with hate as he fumbled at his belt and pulled out his pistol.

Jaske stood frozen.

A rumble and a clatter.

Blackwood had fallen out of bed.

No. He dived out. Scrambled across floorboards on his knees. All in a second. He fell on Orvik and slapped the gun from his hand.

It skittered across the floorboards.

Blackwood clamped a hand on Orvik's mouth but the man writhed away and Blackwood only got his neck. He pressed down hard, trying to strangle him instead.

The Norwegian rolled and bucked under him, a pig at slaughter, kicking and squealing.

Jaske sprang forward and fell on his legs, holding him down. He writhed under her weight and Blackwood's, the Englishman's hands still pressing down on his throat, squeezing the life out of him.

Orvik choked and growled a single word.

"Jaevel."

His eyes bulged with terror. His legs kicked, banging the floor.

This was the moment of death.

The Norwegian thrashed under Blackwood with the paroxysms of a drowning man.

And then he kicked a little less.

And then he didn't move at all.

And then he was dead.

"Shit," said Blackwood. He slumped to the side and fell away, gasping, clutching the wound at his shoulder. A bloom of blood seeping through his shirt.

Jaske clambered to her knees.

Orvik was dead, eyes staring at her still, mouth open in a frozen sneer, like he was delivering a last insult. She looked down at his pathetic cock and balls and glanced across at the scissors lying to the side.

31

JASKE FINGERED THE SCISSORS and snipped them before catching Blackwood's curious look. She almost laughed at the absurdity of it: both of them slumped, panting over the body of a dead man, his genitals out, and a swathe of blood arced across the floor.

Panic. That was what it was.

She stifled her laugh and swallowed her insane, inappropriate grin.

Blackwood slapped his own face. "Shit," he said. "I needed more time."

"More time? For what?"

He shook his head. His eyes glazed. Of course. He was still dazed and reeling from the morphine. And the torture. "We have to get out of here now," he said.

"Now?" Why was she asking dumb questions? Of course they had to get out now. They'd murdered one of the captors. This was it. They had to flee now or be killed.

She nodded and clambered to her feet. He rose too, slower than her, groaning as he staggered and swayed, holding onto the table, and staring at the scattering of medical supplies, as if contemplating more morphine.

Jaske went to the door, like she might walk right out of this place. She peeked through to the bunk room. The two guards standing inside at the far end. They were smirking at the sight of the girls, all cocooned on their bunks, trying to ignore the world. There was no privacy in there.

One of the guards caught sight of her as she peeked through the slit in the door. The smirk fell from his lips. He left his comrade and came marching the length of the bunk room.

"One of them is coming."

Blackwood bent down with another groan and snatched Orvik's pistol. He was going to shoot the Russian as he came through. Wouldn't that alert everyone?

But Blackwood shoved the pistol in his jeans, behind his back, leaned down once more and took the torch from Orvik's belt.

The guard came through as Jaske hid behind the door. He saw Orvik lying on the floor, his pants around his knees, exposed and obscene. The blood.

There was a moment when he gasped. Just a moment. It might have been only a single second.

Blackwood stepped forward, swiped, and smashed the guard's Adam's apple through the back of his neck.

Without thinking of it, Jaske shoved the door closed.

The guard choked a hoarse silent scream as his knees buckled. Blackwood cracked the torch over his skull and he fell like a sack of bricks.

Dull boots stomped the length of the bunk room next door.

The second sentry bundled through the door.

This was a fatal error. He might have run out and alerted everyone; brought the whole army with him.

Jaske still wasn't sure that would have saved him.

Blackwood smashed the torch full across his temple. It broke, scattering plastic and crystal filament across the floorboards. The guard fell forward, tripping over his comrade, and they were both lying unconscious.

Or dead.

Blackwood reached for a black scabbard hanging off the belt of the second guard and pulled out a hunting knife. A 'Storm'. She knew the model. The Russians sold them across the border. They would sell anything.

Blackwood took the knife and put it to his throat.

"No," she said.

He paused, surprised.

"You're going to kill them?" It was an absurd question.

"We don't want them waking and sounding the alarm. We need as much time between us and them as we can get."

She didn't nod or agree or say anything at all. Blackwood stared for a moment and then slit the man's throat. Blood gushed out under him and spread across the concrete floor. He did the same with the first guard and they were both dead.

Jaske felt her knees trembling. He had dispatched three men in a minute and almost without thought. Like she would dispatch fish she'd caught under the ice. You reeled them in and bashed their heads and gutted them with a sharp knife. You made it quick.

But of course, she had always had more thought, more reverence for the animals she'd killed. There was a respect for their life, for the food they gave you. You respected that creature's life by using every part of it so none of it was wasted.

This man didn't give his human victims that respect.

But then, they were monsters. They didn't deserve any respect. She had always thought she could not do this. But she had rammed a pencil through Khryushka's brain. She was the same as Blackwood. It was just that he was the one holding the knife.

She stared as he took a pair of boots and socks off one of his victims and swiftly pulled them over his bandaged feet. He turned the guard over, his eyes staring at the ceiling, blood gurgling from his throat, and unbuckled the man's belt, whipping it off and sliding it round his waist, adjusting it for the pistol he'd already tucked into his jeans. He wiped the knife on the dead man's tunic and slotted it into the scabbard at his waist.

He took the first guard's belt off too and tossed it to Jaske.

"Here, wear this. You know how to shoot a gun?"

She nodded, took the knife out, examined it in the dull yellow light, and glanced at the scissors lying on the floor in all the blood. The pathetic little bandage scissors she'd hoarded as her secret weapon for days. And now she had a hunting knife and a Makarov.

"There's a spare clip in the holster," Blackwood said. "Only eight bullets in the clip, so sixteen in all."

She nodded again. Thirty-two bullets and two knives to get them out of this hell hole and across the border.

Blackwood took his pistol out and slid back the breech in a second, flipping off the safety in one fluid, expert movement. "Let's go."

He pushed through the door and Jaske heard a gasp of surprise from the women.

32

BLACKWOOD TAPPED HIS FINGER to his lips and held the pistol away from himself, palm open, so it sat in the ball of his thumb — the universal *I'm no threat* pose.

The women gasped and one even yelped in shock but they stifled their desire to cry out.

Jaske came through, hooking her belt around her waist. The women caught a glimpse of the carnage in the next room and clamped their hands on their mouths.

"I need you all to be quiet," Blackwood said. "Do you understand me?"

He looked to Jaske, as if she might be his translator, then realized his mistake. These women were Norwegian. They would all speak perfect English. Several of them confirmed it.

"We understand."

"What's happening?"

"You've killed them?"

The last with a haunted sense of wonder.

"Do as he says, Mimmi," Jaske said. "We're getting out of here."

The woman called Mimmi shook her head, clutching her throat. "You're going to get us all killed."

Blackwood scanned their faces, assessing the forces. This was vital in any operation. Who was with you, committed? Who could you rely on? Who was malleable? Who could be swayed and who was a threat? He scanned their faces to detect exactly how many would require persuasion.

The women looked from Mimmi to Jaske and Blackwood. There had been a power struggle that had been festering for some time. He could read it. Mimmi had wrested power from Jaske, that much was clear.

Mimmi was the one he had to sway.

"I'm going to get us all out of here," he said, looking at Mimmi, a thread of cold steel to his voice.

"We either go now," said Jaske, "or we're raped some more and sold off to be raped again."

Every woman glanced involuntarily at one of the women; the only who hadn't got up from her bunk. She sat staring at her feet.

"I'm sorry, Helve," Jaske said. "I didn't mean..."

The woman called Helve rose, brushed wisps of blonde hair from her face, and said, "I'd rather die running than stay here."

All the women looked down at their feet before gritting their teeth. They murmured.

"Yes, let's go."

"Let's go now."

"We need to run."

Mimmi shuddered and shook her head, folding her arms. But she was shame-faced, defeated. A tear rolled down her cheek.

"What's the plan?" Jaske asked.

"The coach," said Blackwood. "It's sitting in the carport just across there. We get in and drive out of here. Can we make it across the border in that thing?"

Jaske chewed her thumb and thought about it, mentally going over the terrain between here and wherever it was they needed to be safe. She looked up and nodded. "Yes."

Blackwood knew, by the tone of her voice, the way that single word was delivered as an intake of breath, that she was lying. It was impossible. But it was all they had.

"At least we have night cover," Blackwood said. "It's twenty yards that way. We sneak out and walk slowly, quietly. I'll go first. Jaske, you stay and bring up the rear. I'll cover you all."

The women scrambled for their clothes, woolly hats, parkas and puffa jackets. Blackwood peeped through the window. No figures silhouetted against the snow. The black square of the carport building out there. No movement, no light from cigarettes or torches. The beat of music and men's voices emanated from a concrete block further down the compound.

Blackwood went to the door and opened it. A blast of cruel wind howled in. He peeped around the corner. All clear. Out at the entrance to the compound, he could see the outline of the guard hut but anyone looking at the camp would see only shadows.

Checking both ways again and holding his breath to listen once more, he stepped out and walked calmly through snow, gently crumping underfoot, heading for the carport building. A nonchalant stroll, nothing furtive. The desultory walk of someone who had a right to be there and had walked from this hut to that carport a thousand times.

He held the Makarov low to his side against his thigh so no one would see the silhouette of a gun.

He made it out of the wind to the cover of the carport building, where the bus sat, a great, silent presence.

Shadows joined him, a line of black figures creeping across those twenty yards of open space.

To the first woman — he couldn't see which one — he said, "Get on board."

She tugged open the door with a squeal of rusty hinge and Blackwood held his breath, focusing on the figure left at the door to the barrack. Jaske.

He gestured to her to follow. She looked both ways, as he had, and then scurried over, faster than all of them, the fear of being left behind chasing her.

The women crept onto the bus. A roar of male laughter sailed on the air. Jaske reached him, ducking into the warm, dark space.

"One thing first," Blackwood said, pointing to the UAZ Hunter jeeps parked in a row. "We need to take care of those."

He drew out his knife and Jaske did the same. They crept around the jeeps and slashed every tire, then jumped on the bus, trying not to trip in the pitch blackness. Blackwood pushed Jaske into the driver's seat and whispered, "You know how to drive one of these?"

"I would if I could see."

He flipped on the torch, keeping it below the dashboard — enough light to gently illuminate the cabin but not to shine outside.

The keys were in the ignition. Of course they were. On a base like this, you couldn't trust the keys to one person and then have to go look for that person when a vehicle was needed. He wondered if he should have taken the keys from the jeeps. No, it would have taken too much time, opening the doors, and the potential noise. Slashing the tires was easier.

The women had crept down the bus and were all crouched low in the aisle or in the seats.

Jaske gritted her teeth and turned the ignition. The bus shuddered and roared into life, so loud it might bring every soldier in the camp. It seemed like a supersonic plane going over, but no one came running. It was perhaps a little noise, and not unexpected.

"Go for it," Blackwood said.

Jaske hit the accelerator and the bus eased out, swerving onto the icy road, and heading for the gate, a hundred yards away.

Blackwood ducked in the stairwell next to Jaske, and pushed open the concertina door, bracing himself on the handrail.

Two figures came out, illuminated by the light from their hut to the side of the gate. From the casual way they shuffled out, Blackwood could see they were only expecting it to be routine. That this was one of their own, perhaps taking the bus back or out somewhere on official business.

Jaske bit her lip and slammed her foot full down on the gas. The bus growled and roared towards them.

About thirty yards out, the sentries stiffened.

They could see this wasn't going to slow down. They could see there was something wrong about this.

They unslung their guns from their shoulders. Kalashnikovs.

The bus ate up the white road between them.

Blackwood leaned out of the open door and braced his shooting arm against the edge of the bus to keep it steady.

He fired off a couple of shots.

The sentries ducked, hesitated, wondering if they should run or stand their ground.

One of them raised his Kalashnikov and set off a hail of bullets.

Too late.

The bus smacked into both of them.

For a moment the sentries plastered the windscreen, frozen photographs of screaming men. Then they crumpled under the wheels. Their broken bodies rumbled down the bus and spat out with the exhaust fumes.

The bus smashed through the gate and they tore down a stretch of dark, open road.

33

THE BUS RUMBLED OVER the road's surface, rutted with permafrost. Blackwood's teeth rattled. How much time did they have before the Russians changed the tires on the jeeps and gave pursuit.

He looked back down the length of the bus through the great open rear window.

Several lights blinked on the road behind.

Jaske squinted at her side mirror.

"What is it?" Blackwood asked. "Cars?"

The lights floated apart, not in pairs.

"No," Jaske said. "Snowmobiles."

They grew larger in the rear view and there was a forlorn burst of gunfire that didn't touch the bus.

The road turned sharp left and Jaske yanked the steering wheel as far as she could. The bus skidded the turn with a squeal of protest and roared on.

Blackwood scooted to the rear of the bus and peered out, gun pointed, to pick as many of them off as he could as they negotiated the turn.

But the snowmobiles sped off the road at an angle and disappeared into the darkness.

"Why are they going that way?" Blackwood barked, running down the aisle.

"They want to take us further down the road," Jaske called, swallowing a sob of despair in her voice. She pointed ahead, her finger tracing a great arc. "The road goes that way."

Blackwood followed her finger. The road veered east and then cut back sharply west, in a great arc. The snowmobiles were cutting across the plain to head them off.

They sped along for what seemed like an age, almost as if they were on an excursion and this was all so normal, just the sense of a great gentle arc, and then they were on a stretch of straight road.

"They're up ahead," Jaske said.

"Put the lights on," he said. "Full glare."

Jaske flipped the headlights on, and the road ahead lit up.

Blackwood could make out the outline of several men a hundred metres ahead.

They'd set up an ambush, fanned out to hit them from different directions. One of them shielded his eyes.

The light had blinded them. It would only be a moment before they dealt with the glare and opened fire.

He pulled open the concertina doors, steeled himself against the side of the bus, took aim and released a couple of shots.

One of them fell.

Turning quickly to the second target, he shot again.

A crackle of machine-gun fire rattled the side of the bus like a rain of pebbles.

Screams.

He couldn't tell if he'd taken out the second one.

The bus roared on.

One of them broke rank and ran into the road, pointing his Kalashnikov right at them.

Blackwood held tight and shot, his arm jolting, missing every time, an urgent desire to empty the entire clip.

"Keep going!" he yelled.

Blackwood shot again.

The bullet winged the soldier in the road and he staggered, his machine-gun spraying the night air.

There was a moment when he glanced back and caught the bus heading right for him, thought about jumping, too late, and the coach smacked into him.

He flew out of the way like a football booted high.

The bus sped on.

Blackwood rammed the door closed and climbed back inside, rushing to the rear of the bus, gun raised ahead of him, ready to shoot out the rear window.

Another crackle of gunfire. He ducked. The rear window shattered, spraying him with glass.

Mimmi stood, yelling. "Stop! Go back! They're going to kill us!"

Blind panic. In a situation like this, there was always one who wanted to set the clock back to normality, even if normality meant death.

Blackwood scooted down the aisle, keeping low.

"Fucking turn the bus around!" she screamed.

"Shut up!" Blackwood barked.

"Don't you order me! They're going to kill us all!"

Blackwood nudged the safety on his Makarov and put the barrel to her forehead. "If you don't shut up, I'll shoot you now and throw you out that window."

She shut her eyes tight. One of the women pulled her into a seat well, where Mimmi cowered, whimpering.

Jaske turned the bus sharp left and they were driving down a barren coast road.

"This is the only road for miles around," Jaske said, as if sensing his thoughts. "We can't go across land. It winds a lot through mountains."

"I thought you knew the shortcuts," he said.

"When we get closer to the border! But I told you. It's about three hours away."

"Shit."

Three hours on an exposed road, being chased by Curtis's private army. He wondered how long it would take them to replace a wheel on one of those UAZ Hunter jeeps. Or all of them. They would be trained. They'd manage it in no time.

"Keep your foot down," he said. "As much as you can."

Jaske nodded. There was no sign that she wanted to slow down at any point.

They seemed to be going down a long, isolated stretch of coast road, a black sea to their right.

Blackwood glanced at the fuel gauge. It was full. At least that was something. Now all he had to worry about was whether there was enough fuel to take them all the way across the border.

He had almost relaxed into the journey when lights flared on the road behind.

34

THE HUNTER JEEPS. Two, maybe more. The road was narrow so it was difficult to tell. They'd replaced the wheels in quick time and pursued. The jeeps were faster than a crappy old LAZ bus and would catch them up in a few minutes.

Jaske swerved the bus sharp right again and the sea was now on the left side, a great black void that threatened to swallow them whole.

The lights behind blazed brighter.

"Jaske, give me your gun," he said.

She checked the rear-view mirror to the side. "Can't reach just now."

He leaned across her, pulled the Makarov from her holster and struggled to unbutton the spare clip. The scent of her against him, suddenly intimate. She leaned away, to see around him. The bus lurched and bumped, the undercarriage scraping the frost.

He pulled the pistol and spare clip free and marched down the aisle to the rear of the bus. The window was big and wide. A great, gaping shark's mouth, with jagged glass teeth. Too wide. No cover. He would have to crouch and pop up to shoot. No time to get a bearing on a target without exposing himself.

They appeared to be driving along a great stretch of lake. It lay just to their side, vast and frozen. One slip and they would be off the narrow road and into the lake.

But the narrowness of the road meant the chasing jeeps couldn't flank them, and could only queue up, one at a time. But as soon as the land either side became manageable, they would attempt to flank the bus. Hunters were all terrain vehicles, but with these conditions, going off-road would be slow.

Two figures popped up behind the driver, standing in the rear well, aiming Kalashnikovs. They unleashed a rain of gunfire.

Blackwood ducked and hoped no bullets would penetrate.

The machine-gun fire ceased. He sprang up and fired off a few rounds. One of the shooters slumped and hung off the side of the jeep, his Kalshnikov hanging from his arm and trailing. It snagged under the wheel and the force yanked him clean off the jeep.

Blackwood ducked again.

He threw away the first clip and slammed the spare from the holster into the handle of the Makarov. Another eight bullets. And sixteen with Jaske's gun.

Any of the three soldiers they'd already killed: if only he'd been able to snatch a Kalashnikov. Anything for a bit of spray-and-pray.

"Can anyone use a gun?" he called.

The women, all cowering in and under the seats stared back, dumbfounded, like he'd said it in Chinese. This was what happened to real people in life-or-death situations. They shut down.

One of them stood. The one called Helve. She staggered to the rear of the bus and held out her hand. Blackwood handed her Jaske's gun.

"Only eight bullets per clip and two clips so be sparing."

Helve went to the rear window and shot off four rounds in two seconds.

Blackwood shoved her down to the floor. Machine-gun fire shredded the roof.

"Helve," he shouted. "Look at me."

She looked up into his eyes. Clear and blue, even in the blackness.

"You have four bullets left in that clip. Make. Them. Count. Understand?"

She nodded.

"I shoot, then you shoot. Okay?"

"Okay," she said.

He sprang up and fired off a round, just to keep them down. The surviving shooter popped up with his machine-gun. In a second or two he'd be firing.

Blackwood took careful, slow aim, trying to steady himself against the sway of the bus. That front wheel, his sole blurred target.

"Now," he said.

Helve stood and shot a single round.

The soldier in the passenger seat whiplashed and slumped on the dashboard, sending a cloud of red over the cracked windscreen.

"Good shot!"

Blackwood slowed his breathing and concentrated on that front wheel.

The soldier in the rear twisted and struggled to hold his Kalashnikov steady, swaying as the jeep juddered over the frozen road.

Blackwood squeezed the trigger.

The front wheel exploded. The jeep jerked, upended, and skimmed off the road.

Two more jeeps behind. Damn it.

Helve jumped up and shot again, cracking the windscreen of the jeep that followed. Blackwood couldn't be sure but it looked like she'd hit someone inside.

He tried to get a fix on the driver, the bus jolting and swaying so erratically, he could barely fix on the ground, let alone the jeep.

Helve shouted a stream of Norwegian.

The women leaped up and started tearing the seats out. The rusty old bolts gave out. Three of them stormed to the rear, screaming, launching a seat like a battering ram. Blackwood ducked away as they threw it out of the rear window.

It bounced on the road, smashed the windscreen of the jeep, and somersaulted clean over, hitting the jeep behind and skittering off.

Another seat went careering out of the back of the bus and crumpled under the wheels of the jeep. The vehicle buckled and swayed and skidded, tumbling over and disappearing into the night.

The women screamed their delight.

Only one didn't join in. The one called Mimmi was behind, still on her knees and praying loudly. Maybe it was helping.

The bus hit a rise in the road and Blackwood looked down on the road behind. There were three jeeps following.

And at that moment, the second jeep veered off the road and onto the land. Was it a beach that ran alongside the road? He couldn't make it out in the darkness, but the jeep had no difficulty with the terrain. It sped ahead and alongside them.

Two men in the back kneeled and aimed their machine-guns.

"Everybody down!" Blackwood screamed.

A fusillade of fire strafed the side of the bus. The windows shattered and showered them with glass.

Three of the women scrambled to their feet, ripped another seat out and hurled it out the side.

The soldiers ducked. One fell back. The jeep swayed and tried to right itself, arcing back so it almost hit the bus.

"Jaske! Ram him!" Blackwood yelled.

Jaske jerked the steering wheel.

There was a great clunk and the jeep spasmed away, spun in a circle and rolled over, down a stretch of bank and plunged through ice into the lake.

Helve at the rear fired off two more rounds till her gun clicked. She ducked and Blackwood slid the spare clip to her. She ejected the old one and rammed in the spare. She'd shot before.

"When I say go, we both get up and shoot. Aim for the tires, okay?"

Helve nodded.

Blackwood counted to three. "Go!"

They sprang up and took aim. The jeep was right on their tail. A sole sentry in the rear, trying to steady himself and take aim. He was pointing downwards, aiming at the wheels of the bus.

Helve and Blackwood fired off a steady stream of bullets. One tire popped and exploded. Helve got it.

Blackwood hit the other.

The jeep jack-knifed and spun on the ice, throwing the soldier in the back clean out. He flew through the air and hit the back of the bus with a great thud.

Blackwood snatched for the Kalashnikov.

Missed it.

The soldier fell in the road. Dead.

The bus sped on. Blackwood held his gun steady on the pursuers. The jeep rolled over onto its roof, silhouetted in the glow from the jeep behind. He expected it to round the stricken jeep and continue the pursuit, but it didn't.

It just stayed there and the light faded as they sped away.

35

"Why have we stopped?" Beria screamed. "They're getting away!"

Curtis gripped the steering wheel, his knuckles white, staring ahead at the wreckage blocking the road.

"Go round!" Beria yelled.

Curtis was pale. Even in this light, Beria could see that he'd turned ashen. A film of sweat on his forehead. Was the big tough SAS veteran having a heart attack? He cast an anxious glance back at his two guards in the rear.

"Are we okay?"

The guards nodded their heads in unison. A slow-motion nodding that was almost out of a dream.

What was this? This English operative who had come with orders from on high, codenamed 'Nepravda' — was he pursuing something purely personal — an agenda that wasn't from Moscow?

"Just what is it you have in the back there?" Beria demanded.

"You're not authorized to know that," Curtis said.

"You fucking..." Beria spluttered, helpless, losing it. What could he say? He jumped out and strode to the upturned jeep, the headlights casting his shadow before him.

The bodies of his soldiers mangled inside. The smell of gasoline and blood. How many men had he lost to that half-dead Englishman and a bunch of girls? It was fucking embarrassing.

Curtis came up to examine the carnage. Far off down the long, dark road, the red lights of the bus faded into the blackness.

"You know," Beria said, "an Englishman with the KGB. It's unconscionable. Deeply unpatriotic."

Curtis wiped his forehead. He was breathing again, the blood coming to his cheeks again. "So is selling submarines and Russian military hardware over the border."

"Perhaps I should make a call to Moscow."

Curtis smirked. "You do that, Beria."

There it was again. That feeling that a tarantula had learned how to text and was sending you messages.

Beria waved his pistol at the red lights in the distance, now disappearing into the blackness. "I can call ahead. I'll have a police unit bring them in."

"You think you can hide that sort of thing?"

Beria holstered his Makarov and turned to the Englishman, looming right into his face; so close he could smell the whisky on his breath. "I could hit them with a warhead and turn this region into another fucking Chernobyl and still no one would know a fucking thing about it! You think I don't control everything that goes on in this godforsaken shithole of a place? A fucking reindeer farts and I know it!"

"Yes," said Curtis. "Of course you do."

Beria watched with helpless fury as Curtis sauntered back to the jeep, got inside, slammed the door, and started the engine. He thought for a moment they might drive off and leave him stranded out here. But Curtis waited, the engine humming.

Beria jutted out his chin, marched back, blinded by the headlights, and got inside.

"We'll follow," Curtis said, and added with a chuckle, "They can't possibly escape, not with your elite squad of crack border patrols."

36

THE ROAD CURVED INLAND, leaving the lake behind and winding over a bleak plain. An icy blast howled through the bus. The women huddled together towards the front, sheltering in the remaining seats.

Blackwood went through them, checking there were no injuries, congratulating them on their work, like a commanding officer geeing up the troops before another onslaught.

They were all fine. No worries.

"I think Mimmi's been hit," one of them said, fighting back sobs.

She was slumped in her seat, her Parka puffed up around her, whimpering like a dog you'd put out of its misery.

Blackwood leaned in to examine her. A neat circle of red on her abdomen. He leaned her forward and she moaned. A larger mass of blood on her back, the size of a dinner plate.

"Looks like it's gone straight through. We need to press on the wound."

"Here!" Jaske called, pointing to the dashboard. "There's a medical box."

At the front of the bus, a compartment with a green cross transfer. One of the women retrieved a plastic box and opened it. There was wadding and tape.

They unzipped Mimmi's Parka and eased it off her, lifting her sweater to expose the wounds, oozing thick blood. They stuffed them with wadding and taped them fast.

The icy wind howled through the broken windows.

"Keep her warm," Blackwood said.

They wrapped her Parka round her. Helve donated her own Puffa jacket, which they draped over Mimmi's knees.

Helve didn't seem worried about the cold. She held onto the Makarov pistol. Blackwood thought it best not to ask for it back. He joined Jaske and leaned in close.

"It won't be enough. That First Aid kit is for bumps and knocks, not Kalashnikov wounds. If we don't get her to a hospital soon, she's dead."

Jaske nodded and put her foot down a little more. The LAZ barely responded. It was working flat out. If she pushed it any more it would give up on them. It was a miracle their bullets hadn't hit the fuel tank.

The fuel gauge showed a third of the gasoline now used up.

Something blinked in the rear-view mirror.

A pair of headlights way behind them.

"They're coming again" Blackwood said.

He marched to the rear to get a closer look.

A pair of headlights winking in the black void. It had to be the Hunter jeep. Probably containing Curtis. He would have taken up the rear and watched his henchmen fall one by one. That was his style.

Blinking as the light blurred, Blackwood tried to calculate how far it was behind and at what rate it was gaining. Maybe a mile away. It didn't seem to be getting any closer. It seemed to be receding.

He went back to Jaske.

"We're losing them," she said.

"Why are they hanging back?" Blackwood asked.

"Maybe you hit them. Their fuel tank is gone. Or a tyre."

It was possible. But the lights looked to be maintaining the same distance. They were tracking now.

"You don't think?" Jaske asked.

"Yeah," he said. "Maybe that's it."

The lights disappeared. Had they shut them down so they could speed up and catch them without signalling their position?

They blinked on again.

No. It was the twists and turns in the road that obscured them. The hilly terrain. They were still tailing.

"Look," Jaske said, nodding forward.

Lights ahead. Not a vehicle approaching. A straight snaking line of light. It was a road. A road lit by streetlamps.

"It's the E105," Jaske said.

The promise of civilisation. Perhaps that was why they were hanging back, afraid to attack where there might be witnesses. But Blackwood didn't think it likely.

The bus wound out of the track and turned into the highway with its bright streetlamps. A sign read *Titovka*. They surged on towards a cluster of lights in the distance.

Some kind of truck stop. Lorries were pulled in. A huddle of huts and shacks. Farmyard vehicles and trucks. A motel sign. There was even a bus stop.

Blackwood laughed at the idea of someone flagging them down. Just a normal bus with all the windows blown out, riddled with bullet holes, and twenty freezing women escaping traffickers.

They sailed through, the streetlights gave out and the road was dark again, just the headlights of the bus lighting a twenty-metre pool before them.

That same pair of eyes following a kilometre behind.

Jaske pointed at a blue road sign.

"Kirkenes, one hundred and twenty," she said.

Blackwood caught the list of other names on the sign as it flashed by. *Linhammar*. Where had he heard that before?

It went on and on, just a two-lane road. This was the artery that ran down Europe, north to south. The *Crimea Highway*. This must be the northernmost stretch of road where it levelled off and ran east to west.

Blackwood blinked and rubbed his eyes, to keep himself awake. The long, dead road was hypnotic.

"You okay?" he said. "Not tired?"

"I'm fine," Jaske said. "You look like shit, though. Have a sleep."

He shook his head. Not with those following. Not with any amount of potential dangers ahead. Not till they were safe.

They arced down a gentle hill towards a pool of light in a valley.

"Sputnik," Jaske said.

"A town?"

"Village."

"How do you know this side of the border so well?"

"We Sámi people don't recognize the border. Norway, Finland, Russia. It's all our land."

Blackwood nodded, not understanding. Might they have radioed ahead for the military or the police to intercept them? There was nowhere safe. Not this side of the border. There was no one that couldn't be bought.

Just outside the village, the streetlamps lined the road on the left side again. As they trundled through, he noticed what looked like government buildings to the left, a tank on a plinth — perhaps a monument to some past conflict — then the buildings petered out and so did the streetlamps.

They rumbled on for a half hour or so as the road twisted and turned through hills. More lights ahead. Another town. A sad, solitary sign said *Pechenga*.

"Pechenga. That's what you said."

"This is where we try to get off the road," Jaske said.

The road became a solid two-lane highway lined with crash barriers as they skirted the town and then the crash-barriers gave up and it was back to being a track through the blackness.

A pair of red eyes stared bright ahead. A white cross beneath them.

A level crossing. There was no barrier, only the light to warn cars not to cross.

"There's a train coming," Jaske said.

Blackwood checked behind. He couldn't see them following, but if they waited here, they would soon catch up. "Keep driving."

Jaske glanced at him but said nothing. She put her foot down and the bus roared on.

37

A WAIL THROUGH THE night air. The unmistakable sound of a train. Blackwood twisted, trying to see behind. The light of a train behind them, the track running alongside the road. He glanced back at the red lights ahead, trying to calculate the speed of the train against the bus.

"Faster!" he hissed.

"My foot's all the way down," Jaske protested.

"Damn."

The train was eating up the space behind them. It wailed again.

Jaske glanced back and saw it. She checked the road ahead and gasped. "We won't make it."

Blackwood tried to calculate how long the bus was. They could make the crossing, but the train might smash the rear of the bus clean off.

The women were all at the front of the bus, but it didn't matter. If the train hit the back of the bus, it would likely kill them all.

The train veered away from them and seemed to be taking a different route, but only to arc back so it could cross the road.

Jaske let out a low groan and hunched her shoulders forward, trying to push the bus on.

This was it. There was no pulling up now. Even if she slammed on the brakes, they would be across the tracks. It was hell or bust.

The train righted itself and came at them at an angle. It wailed again.

Jaske's groan became an animal roar. She closed her eyes. The women behind realized what was happening and all screamed.

The bus hit the tracks and rolled right through.

Blackwood looked back as the train flashed by the shattered rear window. He thought he caught the face of a shocked passenger.

They roared through and Jaske hit the brakes.

The bus screeched to a stop twenty yards up the road.

The train wailed off into the black night.

The screaming stopped and left only weeping in its wake.

"Don't stop," said Blackwood.

Jaske considered the road to the left and one to the right that itself split immediately to two tracks. "That way," she said, jerking the bus sharp east and down an unnamed track road.

She put the lights on and illuminated a narrow track lined with trees on both sides. It was almost like a tunnel.

"What are you doing?" Blackwood asked.

"If we stay on the road, we hit the border and border guards. This way we can cross the border unseen."

"You know a way across that's unguarded?"

She nodded.

"There's no border fence?"

"There *is* no border. Not out here. They used to put in wooden poles but the ice spits them out."

"So we can just ride right across to Norway?"

"Kind of," she said. "I just never did it in a bus before."

"Is that going to be a problem?"

"We'll see," she said.

Blackwood noted the knot of concern on her brow and for the first time worried about what lay ahead.

"What is it?"

She sighed. "The actual border is about eight kilometres right ahead."

"And you're sure there's no checkpoint?"

"Dead sure." She smiled at Blackwood's frown. "It's a river and there's no bridge."

"Then how the hell are we getting across?"

"We drive. The river is iced over."

"Can it hold the weight of this coach?"

She shrugged. "We'll find out."

Jaske flipped the lights off and for a moment they were driving blind through the blackness, but then the snow illuminated the track ahead with an eerie blue glow, just enough to see by.

"There are buildings nearby. Just a few here and there. At this time of year, the border police don't really look for much. But our lights might be noticed."

He checked the fuel gauge again and noted with alarm that it had dropped to below half.

Blackwood turned at a murmuring behind. Helve was leading the women in prayer. It was better than screaming. To his surprise, he recognized it as the Lord's prayer.

Vår Far i himmelen...

Gi oss i dag vårt daglige brød...

Jaske wound the bus along the winding track and they came through a wide-open crossroads where he sensed the faint outline of buildings in the darkness, then they pushed on through a few miles of track with trees hemmed in tight on both sides. What would happen if someone came driving towards them? Blackwood thought about holding them up, transferring everyone to their vehicle and reversing onwards.

They passed through another crossroads, no more than a clearing in the forest, and Jaske said, "It's here."

She drove on another 200 metres and stopped. The forest went right up to the bank. It was hard to see it was a river. There had been a bridge once, but now there was just a dip in the road. Not too steep. Just a gulley that cut through the track.

Jaske eased the bus forward and it tilted down the slope.

This was where they would find out if the ice could hold them, or if they might plunge straight through to the riverbed.

"Ladies," Blackwood called back. "Keep praying."

A metallic clunk reverberated through the bus as the fender hit the ice, and then the front wheels settled. The bus juddered down the slope and then righted itself on the river.

Jaske eased the accelerator, pulsing it, pushing the bus forward in little jerks. The ice creaked and groaned.

Blackwood noticed the women were holding tight to the seats, as if trying to push the bus on. His own fists white on the chrome rail. He was doing it too.

The bus wheels found the opposite bank, which opened out wider than the one behind them. An easier slope to climb.

Jaske pushed the coach forward and it groaned in pain, the engine growling. The head of the bus reached the bank and climbed it.

Something hit the rear with a great crackle and Blackwood ducked instinctively. But it wasn't machine-gun fire. He crept down the aisle. Another great shattering sound and the rear wheels skidded. The bus lurched backwards. The ice. They'd cracked the ice. Blackwood retreated.

Jaske hit the accelerator and leaned forward, teeth gritted, as if she could push the bus forward with her strength.

The bus shuddered and shook.

"Everyone to the front!" Blackwood shouted.

The women scrambled up the aisle and crowded to the front of the bus with a strange calm.

The coach lifted and tilted forward. Another almighty shudder and they lurched forward up the bank. With a squeal, the engine sputtered and the wheels found traction, skidded, slid this way and that, and then juddered forward onto the road.

"We're through. We're on the Norwegian side."

The women screamed relief. Jaske put her foot down and drove the bus on. Another long, winding track through forest, no different to the Russian side. The women hugged each other and laughed and cried.

Blackwood caught Jaske's grim expression and remembered what she'd said about the escape. *Two hours to the border, but another hour or more to the nearest Norwegian town. Only there are we safe.*

They were not out of the woods yet.

38

Once the private reached the forest, he slowed to a brisk march, keeping undercover. There were several vast lakes that he skirted and he could sense himself veering too far south.

The drone of Russian helicopters followed him, scanning the forest. Jets occasionally streaked across the sky, roaring terror, and he cringed and spasmed at the memory of their devastation. Maxwell, Haines and Benson gone. The Sámi guide too. The Chinook crew, the Norwegian crews. All obliterated. Only him left.

Were they looking for him, or were the Russians simply on edge due to the NATO manoeuvres on their border? Or did the Russians now know that NATO forces had encroached Russian air space, crashed and engaged in battle?

He told himself again and again that no one knew he was alive. He just had to keep going till he reached the border. He had to avoid capture.

When he'd circled a vast lake, he came to a narrow track lined with trees on both sides and used it to guide himself west. Keeping twenty yards to the side of the path, he found he could follow it and remain hidden to any helicopter passes.

Eventually, the path opened out to a crossroads. Buildings in the distance. Dogs barked.

A search party following, tracking him?

No, the dogs were coming from the buildings — a compound of some sort. Maybe military. It must all be military out here.

He thought for a wild moment of sneaking in and stealing food. His belly roared with desire. But no. He'd be caught so easily. The dogs would be all over his scent.

He sprinted across the twenty yards of open road and plunged back into the forest again.

Keep running. Putting as much space between those dogs as he could.

He pushed on through, keeping the path to his left. He had been running and walking, stumbling, staggering, for almost a day now. There had been just the three hours of meagre daylight and now all was night. His watch told him it was sixteen hours since the crash.

He came to another crossroads, but not as big as the previous one. This one was little more than a clearing in the forest. He crouched still and silent in the undergrowth, listening, looking both ways, till he was absolutely sure no one was around, then he walked across the open path.

No one at all. Just the chirping of birds.

Welcome forest again.

As he trudged on through the bracken and tangle of roots around his feet, he was aware of a roaring sound ahead. A road?

No, a continuous roar, more like the hum of a motorway, unrelenting. There was no road like that out here.

The roar increased as he pushed on about 200 yards, and the forest stopped.

A river.

The forest went right up to the bank. There had been a bridge once, but there was just a dip in the road. Not too steep. Just a gulley that cut through the track.

In the ground, a wooden post, painted scarlet; a forlorn marker, crooked, as if the earth was spitting it out. On the opposite bank a similar post, striped red and green.

The border. This was the fucking border. He'd made it.

He looked both ways. There were no guards, no patrols, no fences. Just a river and two markers as a warning.

What was it he'd heard? The permafrost spat out any fence they tried to build here. Even concrete posts. The land didn't want it.

He fell down and plunged his face in the water, gasping at the sudden shock of coldness. He took a long, cool slake of water and fought the urge to lay down and sleep.

He plunged into the river, gasping, almost yelling out at the shock of ice, and swam for it. Just a few yards across.

He pounded, stroking with a fury. I will not fucking die here in this godforsaken place. I will cross this fucking border.

He clawed the opposite bank and dragged himself out of the icy flow. Twenty or thirty yards downstream of where he'd dived in.

He pulled himself up the bank, his clothes heavy.

Shivering, he trudged on, giving himself the luxury of the path now that he was on Norwegian soil, knowing that sooner or later he'd come to civilization of some sort.

Within a half hour on the long road, he halted at the sight of a border station. *Korpfjell Grensestasjon.* It must be if his memory of the map was right. He panicked for a moment, thinking maybe he was still on the Russian side and was now captured.

Guards came running towards him, machine guns pointed. Shouting orders.

"Stoppe! Opp med hendene!"

He raised his hands in the air.

Green camouflage. Badges on their breast with a familiar yellow/red coat of arms and the word *Politi.* They were Norwegian border guards.

He was almost too exhausted to grin in triumph. He fell face down in the long dead road.

39

Blackwood noticed Jaske wasn't celebrating. Still that frown.

He leaned close and murmured, "What is it? Are we really on the Norwegian side?"

She glanced in the rear-view mirror that allowed her to see the passengers. "Yes, but it means nothing. We have to get to a town or they will take us in the hinterland."

"How far to a town?"

"It's over an hour east to Hesseng."

Blackwood nodded and calculated their chances. An hour of driving through isolated dirt track like this, with the petrol gauge now in the red and the bus shuddering protest. If it broke down, they'd be stranded, sitting ducks for Curtis and his army, surely little more than a kilometre behind them.

The bus pushed on up the narrow track through forest, rising through hills. It slipped and slid at certain bends. A bleak and lonely stretch.

It might be Norway, Blackwood thought, but Jaske was right. Curtis and his army could come across the non-existent border and kill them right on this track and no one would know.

After an hour, the track spilled out at a junction where a cluster of buildings sat. What looked like a church and a school. A wider road. Gritted. Streetlamps. The wheels eased onto the road like slumping into a warm bed after a day labouring.

"This is Tårnet," Jaske said.

She punched the steering wheel, let out a muffled sob and squealed through gritted teeth.

"What's the matter?" Blackwood asked, scanning the dashboard for a sign something had gone wrong, petrol or oil running out or the fuel gauge broken.

"We're on Route 886," she said.

Not despair. Triumph. She knew they'd escaped.

Blackwood allowed himself a glance back — not at the women squealing and screaming and hugging each other

— but through the rear window, checking for the tell-tale sign of headlights in the gloom.

It appeared no one was behind them.

They trundled on down the luxurious expanse of the two-lane road till it ended at a T-junction with the E105. A wall of yellow and blue road signs for a border point to the left.

"That's *Storskog grensestasjon*. That's the border point we should have come through. Always manned."

Jaske veered right and the lights of the border station faded in the rearview mirror.

Blackwood allowed himself a mental fist pump. Jaske had somehow crossed from Russia to Norway like the border wasn't there.

40

THE LONG, WINDING ROAD through dense forest ended and the two Hunter jeeps pulled up. Beria simmered in the seat next to Curtis, trying to keep a lid on the rage boiling within.

The glow of civilization ahead, streetlamps silhouetting a few angular buildings. Norwegian design. Mocking him.

"It's worrying how they've crossed from Russia to Norway like the border isn't there," Curtis said.

"You've let them ride right into Norway," Beria spat. "You did this!"

Curtis scoffed and consulted his tablet on the steering wheel, his face glowing with the white light. "It was your remarkable lack of Russian border guards, I think."

He didn't seem to care, as if this was all a joke to him. What game was he playing?

Beria leaned over. They had reached a hamlet called Tårnet. There was a church and a school; a few buildings scattered down the highway and not much else. "This is it. We're back to where we were. They're riding home in a Russian bus full of Russian bullets. Do you know what this means, you fool?"

Curtis shrugged. "What if they do find Russian bullets in the bus. What does it prove? Russian hardware is sold both sides of the border. Everyone knows it. It could be Norwegian kids shooting up a Russian bus for sport. I'm sure there'll be an internet conspiracy theory saying exactly that tonight. It will be all over Twitter and Facebook that the real story is being covered up by Norway."

"Bah, fucking Twitter!" Beria said. "This is how you wage a war now?"

Curtis laughed.

Beria turned and glared at the two in the back, daring them to laugh with him. He would take out his Makarov and shoot both of them dead right here if they did. Neither dared.

"Do you know how many people we have pushing whatever Moscow wants people to believe? Are you even aware of that? You sit here in this backwater thinking you're the king of the reindeer but there are armies of your countrymen planting stories all over the world. Telling the world what to think. Soldiers like us, we're redundant now. The real armies are sitting at computers, telling the world what to think. If I say arsenic is an aphrodisiac that the French government has been hiding from its citizens, tomorrow a million Frenchmen will fight for their right to drink arsenic. That's the power I have."

He turned to his guards in the back and nodded. That was all. As if something telepathic had passed between them. They jumped out and changed the license plates on the jeep, slotting the magnetic Norwegian plates over the Russian ones. The jeep was unmarked and none of the men wore identifying uniforms. To all intents and purposes, they were a group of Norwegians on a late-night excursion.

"I don't give a fuck about your army of keyboard warriors," Beria said. "We could have taken that bus easily before they crossed the border," Beria said.

Curtis looked at his tablet and pretended not to hear. Then, just when Beria snorted with impatience, he answered. "A half-dead British ex-soldier and a group of frightened Norwegian girls killed all your men. Perhaps they've been lazing on their arses being smugglers for too long."

"I think you underestimate the tenacity of the Russian military," Beria snapped.

"I think you got your arses kicked in Afghanistan by a bunch of fucking goat herders."

"As did you. It was we Russians who warned you: don't go into Afghanistan, it will be your graveyard."

Curtis said nothing, just looked at him like a reptile looks at a fly out of reach.

Beria sighed and rubbed the knot between his eyes. "Now do you have any ideas regarding the present situation, or are we going to go over whose army has the biggest fuck-ups in history?"

Curtis chuckled and seemed human for the first time. "You have me there. Both our armies have a talent for turning colossal fuck-ups into glorious defeats."

His men jumped in the rear again.

"There are less public ways of getting what we want," Curtis said, taking out his mobile. He tapped a few digits, placed the phone on the dashboard and turned on the speaker phone. A metallic dial tone filled the cabin.

Den Bla Vesken answered, with a shuffling static, a muffled sonorous cacophony. He was walking away from someone, getting out of earshot.

"Yes?" he said.

"Good evening," Curtis said, "Or is it morning? I have no fucking clue with this 24-hour darkness."

"What do you want? Now is not a good—"

"A situation has arisen," Curtis said. "We're on the Norwegian side. At a little pisshole in the snow called Tårnet."

There was a hissing static on the other end that sounded like a plane taking off. It was Bla Vesken breathing hard. "Are you joking? You want to start an international incident?"

"It wouldn't be the first time this has happened," Curtis said.

"Why are you here?" Bla Vesken said eventually.

"It seems our women have escaped. I'm sure you're going to see it on the news any minute now."

The plane taking off hit Mach 1.

"What the fuck? You let them go?"

"I said they escaped."

Bla Vesken let out an animal moan. "You fucking fools. You botched up their sale. You brought them back here, and now you've let them escape!"

Curtis let him rage and moan a little more, a strange, sardonic smile on his lips.

"The women aren't important. We'll take the hit on that. We want the Englishman. He knows where the money is. You want the money, don't you?"

"Jesus. Yes. Of course."

"Well, the man who knows where the money is, he's now on your side of the border."

"What the fuck do you expect me to do about that?"

"I expect you to help us secure him."

"We trade shit across the border," Bla Vesken hissed. "I never agreed to anything like this."

"You agreed to this when you tipped us off to twenty girls on an excursion. You're part of this. Do you understand me?"

There was nothing but static again, and what sounded like a police siren passing.

"Yes," came Bla Vesken's voice.

"Find the Englishman. If you can't deal with him, let us know so we can deal with him."

"Russians, this side of the border, murdering an Englishman. Do you know what kind of international incident this could cause?"

"Yes," said Curtis. "I know exactly." He jabbed at his phone on the dashboard and hung up. The screen showed a map. "He's in Kirkenes."

Beria leaned over to look. A blue dot north of the centre of Kirkenes marked Den Bla Vesken's location.

"Let's join him," Curtis said.

41

THE FUEL GAUGE HAD dropped to empty but the beat-up Russian bus sped on along a lonely highway — the E105, the signs said — with no civilisation but for what looked like a giant shed, its wooden panels illuminated by bright floodlight, a slanted roof forming a portico. A roadside restaurant.

Jaske sped on and everyone looked longingly as they passed, all wondering at the absurd notion of people free to pull in and eat. Normal life was here.

At Elvenes they crossed an arched bridge and sailed through a tunnel, lit up all eerie and spectral with ribs of blue light, like they were sailing through the belly of a whale.

"She's cold."

Tonje was holding Mimmi's hand and staring at it in horror.

"She's cold," she said again.

She put her fingers to Mimmi's wrist, checking the pulse. She looked around wildly, as if one of them had hidden it.

"Oh god, she's dead."

She burst into tears and slapped Mimmi's hand.

Blackwood went over and leaned across to checked Mimmi's neck. There was no pulse at all. She wasn't breathing. She'd gone.

"Leave her," he said.

Tonje crept away into the arms of a friend and wept.

Blackwood took the puffa jacket someone had lent her and placed the hood over her face. Some of the other women were weeping. He wondered if he should say anything, but there was nothing to be said.

Helve stared with no emotion at all, the Makarov pistol on her knee.

They skirted a village and a yellow sign for Kirkenes startled Blackwood. It gave the name in Russian too and he thought again they might have drifted back across to the Russian side. Why did he not feel safe?

Jaske said, as if reading his mind, "The Russians come across the border to shop and trade. It's an invasion, but of shoppers."

The highway led to a headland that twinkled with promising light. A little town out there.

"This is where we stop. I'm thinking we get them to Kirkenes. It's a town. They will be safe... for now."

Blackwood noted that she didn't include herself in that.

She sped along a highway that skirted a lake. It seemed every road here edged water, as if there was hardly any land at all. They came to the town and an illuminated sign at the side of the road, high up on a bank, said *Velkommen til Kirkenes*.

Jaske tore down the E6 main road that circled the town, the engine groaning and squealing in protest. People passing looked up from tramping through snow to stop and wonder at this sight of a Russian bus with bullet holes and broken glass.

Jaske pulled the bus into a square where Christmas lights hung and a Christmas tree stood, illuminated. Snow and slush everywhere. The engine screamed in protest.

Shoppers stopped and stared and some approached, curious to see what this Russian bus with all its windows smashed was all about.

Jaske killed the engine and it spluttered and died like it couldn't have gone another yard. She leapt out of the driver's seat, yanked open the door and stumbled out to the square. The women filed out after her, leaving Mimmi sitting in her seat, a puffa jacket over her face.

As Helve passed, Blackwood took her arm.

"Best not go out with that," he said.

She looked down at the Makarov in her hand as if wondering how it got there, or maybe how she might not take it with her, as if it had become her hand.

She nodded and took in a deep breath, stifling a sob, gritted her teeth, nodded again, steeling herself.

She let him take the gun. He pocketed it swiftly.

Outside, Jaske jumped up onto the plinth of a statue and shouted a string of Norwegian.

There were gasps from the growing crowd, women shrieked and covered their mouths; some took their phones out and started filming.

Blackwood stayed out of sight, sitting on the steps of the bus.

Jaske stood on some kind of war memorial. A bronze of a woman holding a baby. A boy sitting at her feet in a snowdrift, gazing off into the distance, like a dazed bomb victim. Maybe it was a girl with short hair.

Plenty were filming on their phones. Shrieks and moans of shock from the crowd. These were the kidnapped girls everyone had been talking about.

Jaske switched to English. She was making sure the story went international.

"We were on an excursion to Sámi hunting grounds when we were kidnapped. I say now, the band of criminals who took us were both Norwegian and Russian. We were taken to a military camp in Russia, just over the border. It was a combined operation between Russian and Norwegian criminals and there were military personnel on both sides. They are smuggling goods across the border and we kidnapped women were part of that!"

It was quite possible this was going out live to a shocked nation, a shocked world.

Blackwood ducked out of the bus. It was time to go. He dodged round the back of the bus, keeping to the shadows.

"We escaped by killing several guards and taking their weapons! We crossed the border in this Russian bus we stole from the military camp where we were held captive! Russian soldiers are involved in this, but I say again, so were Norwegians! I'm sure if you examine the bullets in the bus, you will find they are Russian calibre. One of our group was shot and killed in the escape. She is the only casualty."

Jaske was talking to the nation, making it clear what was happening. She was setting the story.

The nasal whine of a police siren complained a few streets away.

Blackwood sauntered off, his hands on the Makarovs in his pockets, keeping to the shadows.

No one saw him duck away into the nearest alley and disappear.

42

A POLICE CAR CAME into the square, blue lights revolving and whirling over the snow-covered square, competing with the Christmas lights.

Jaske wondered if Christmas had happened. She'd lost track.

The crowd around them parted and Jaske stepped down off the statue.

A gaggle of cops, fat and ponderous. The officer in charge with bugged out eyes, like he couldn't believe what he was seeing. A bombed out Russian bus and ten refugee women destroying the cute calm of this Christmas scene.

"Is this right?" the head cop said. "You are the kidnapped University girls?"

"We are," Jaske said. "We escaped."

His men were already trying to bat down people's phones, and people were telling them to fuck off. Like they could stop anyone filming this.

"I'm Inspector Eriksen," he said. "You're safe now."

The shock on his face. A blundering local border cop, so out of his depth he was wading in lead boots.

"Stop filming!" he yelled.

"Fuck you!" someone shouted back.

"There's no law against it."

"Who do you think you are?"

It was too late for him to do anything about it, Jaske could see. People in the crowd were probably already uploading their videos to YouTube, some had probably been streaming it live. Everything she'd said was already out there in the world. No one could suppress it.

Eriksen gazed on the shot-up bus with wonder, like he was totting up how much paperwork this would involve, and how much of an international incident he might be up to his fat neck in.

"We were chased over the border by Russian military," Jaske said. "I have no doubt they'll come right here and shoot you all to take us back. You need to get these girls out of here. to Tromsø or somewhere safe. They wouldn't dare move on Tromsø."

"I know what to do, thank you, miss," he said.

But he glanced all about him as if he was looking for someone to tell him what to do.

"One of the girls is dead. She's on the bus. They shot her during the escape."

Eriksen went pale. Even in the sickly yellow Christmas light, she could tell.

Within a half hour, maybe even only a quarter hour, a coach came and they asked the girls all to get on board. An ambulance came too and they took Mimmi's body off and carried her away.

Jaske stayed with the police inspector. It seemed she was different, as she always had been. The Sámi tour guide, not one of the innocent Norwegian girls. She was going to be treated very differently.

"Was there anyone else with you?" Eriksen asked.

"No."

"You escaped all by yourself, without any help?"

"That's right."

"You need to come in for questioning."

"I'd like to go home and see my family."

"We need to talk to you. You can't. You just can't."

"Am I being arrested?"

"Do you know how many officials and agencies are going to descend on this place now? If I tell them I let you go, how do you think that will look?"

"Okay," she said. "May I go to the bathroom?"

"What?"

"I've been driving that bus for three hours and if you don't let me go, I'm going to piss myself right here."

Eriksen flapped his arms in protest, as if she'd asked him to conjure a bathroom from his backpack. He looked around the square and spied the bar down the street off the square.

"There," he said. "The A1 Pub. Go there."

"Thanks," she said, already setting off.

"You! Go with her."

One of the policemen shrugged and sighed and followed her, trudging behind her in the snow.

Jaske glanced around the square as she walked, looking for Blackwood's face, but it seemed he'd disappeared.

43

It was the kind of cool bar that had made an effort before the hipsters came along and thought any old random shit would do. There was a row of elegant booths by the Venetian-blinded windows, tasteful seating units and bar stools, all chrome, dark pine and charcoal.

Heads turned when she came in and Jaske was conscious that she probably looked a total mess, like a homeless woman or something. And with a cop in tow.

They were whispering and chatting and it was obvious that the news that had hit the square had quickly filtered through to the bar. She was a celebrity.

She turned to the cop and said, "I need to call my mother."

The cop shook his head. "I can't let you do that."

"Come on," she said. "I just returned from being kidnapped. Let me tell my mother I'm alive." Tears sprang to her eyes and she let a flurry of sobs spill out of her.

"I don't know." The cop looked over his shoulder as if he expected Eriksen to be there to tell him what to do.

"Let her call her mother, man!" The barman placed his mobile phone on the bar. "You can use my phone, girl."

"Bloody cops, man!" someone shouted.

"All right," the policeman said, "but be quick."

She took the phone, blinking tears from her eyes and muttering a 'Thank you,' through sobs to the barman.

She had to think of the number. She'd memorised it, just for these kinds of moments when your mobile phone was lost or stolen and you needed to call that emergency number; that person you could rely on.

She tapped in the digits and put the phone to her ear.

On a TV above the bar, a news reporter was already suggesting that the missing Norwegian girls might have been found. Reports unconfirmed. Guys in the bar looked from the TV to her with strange smiles. Some toasted each other. She was about to become the good news story of the holidays.

The electronic bleat cut off and a voice said, "Yeah?"

She turned from the cop and whispered low. "Anda. It's me. Jaske."

Her brother gasped and bombarded her with a flurry of questions.

"Listen. Come get me. Now. Behind the A1 Pub. Can you do that?"

"You're in Kirkenes?"

"Right now."

"Yeah," he said. "I'm coming."

She hung up and handed the barman his phone.

She really did have to go to the bathroom. A sharp pain in her side, she'd held on so much.

She hooked her thumb to the neon sign that said *Kvinner.* The cop waved her on and went back to staring at the TV. Jaske passed a billiard table and sauntered through to the toilets.

Closing herself in a cubicle, she wiped her eyes and pissed like a reindeer, the pain in her side easing. Such a relief.

She came out and examined her face in the mirror. Her eyes rimmed black, hair greasy, a bruise luminous purple on her cheek, a cut above her right eye, lips chapped and the corners of her mouth white and cracked.

She looked a fucking mess.

She stepped out of the bathroom and was about to check if the cop could see her. A figure bundled her away, lifted her feet clean off the floor, hand over her mouth.

Her scream caught in her throat and was nothing but a muffled groan. Not now, not after all this and so close to home.

Cold air hit her and the man whispered, "Don't scream."

It was Blackwood. He took his hand from her mouth.

"I thought you'd gone," she croaked.

"Where would I go?"

"I've called my brother. He's here in Kirkenes. He's coming to pick me up."

Blackwood smiled, and something soared in her heart. It was what he'd have done.

"Good thinking. You don't want the police to take you. You'll be their property for a long time, and between you and me, I wouldn't trust them."

The cop in the bar. He wouldn't wait too long before he came looking for her.

"You think they're involved in this?" she asked.

"No. I think they're incapable of protecting you. Curtis and his gang followed us here. They let us go. They want me and they'll use you to get to me."

"So the best thing you could do is disappear," she said, but as she said it she knew she didn't want him to do that.

"I would. If I thought it would help. But they'll still come for you. They'll think you know something. They'll kill you for it and everyone you know."

She bit her lip. This was serious. She was back home, but even here they could get her. He was right.

"We need to go. That way," she said.

He gripped her elbow and marched her down the pedestrianised street, a row of shops. She waited for the bark of a cop to stop them.

They reached the road where cars were parked and turned the corner, purely to get out of sight if that cop did come storming out of the pub's back door. Jaske halted and looked up and down.

A police car sped up the street, blue light flashing, and Blackwood turned to her and huddled in a shop doorway.

It passed and turned up the street, no doubt heading for the square.

A car with a squealing clutch came trundling after it. She recognized the sound.

"It's my brother." She couldn't stop herself smiling. "Come on," she said, "let's get out of here."

44

BLACKWOOD GOT IN THE back seat, while Jaske leaped in the passenger seat and hugged the driver. A few breathless words he couldn't make out and then she urged him to drive away.

He sped off down the narrow back street and swerved away, the clutch squealing, and in a moment was heading out of town the way they'd entered.

He was a boy, a teenager, holding back tears of joy. He changed gears and patted Jaske's knee. She gripped his gloved hand till he had to change gear again and he rattled on in something that sounded Norwegian but nothing Blackwood recognized. It was all rolling Rs and clipped vowels.

"English," Jaske said, turning to Blackwood in the back. "This is my brother, Anda." It sounded like *Onder*.

Anda glanced back at Blackwood and took him in, suspicious.

"This is..." She floundered. "Blackwood."

"John," he said.

"John," said Jaske, tasting the word for the first time. "John helped us escape. He was also a prisoner."

"Okay," Anda said, with a pronounced American inflection. "Thank you for rescuing my sister."

The car pulled out of the town past the *Velkommen til Kirkenes* sign and headed down the highway they'd come along only an hour before in that rattling, freezing, bullet-riddled bus. The stingy drizzle of air from the heater felt like the blast of heat you got when you stepped off a plane in Africa.

"So the whole country has been talking about it," Anda continued. "University class kidnapped on excursion to the Sámi outerlands. It's a big scandal. Some people are blaming the Norwegian government and its treatment of us Sámi people. Others are saying it's the Sámi who kidnap nice Norwegian girls and sell them to Arabs."

"Anyone talking about Russia?" Blackwood asked.

"Pah. You can say it but as soon as you do you get a thousand trolls hitting your post, trying to close your account. Fucking bots, man. Half the country now thinks we Sámi did it."

"It was Russians," said Jaske. "And Norwegians with them."

Anda punched the steering wheel. "Fucking *fitten!*"

That word again. The Norwegians had shouted it at the women. *Fitte*. And at Jaske it was *Sámi fitte*.

"I made sure I shouted the truth in the square just now," said Jaske, "and people were filming it. It'll be on social media now, I guess."

"Why are you hiding from the police?"

Jaske looked at Blackwood.

"We don't know if we can trust them," Blackwood said.

"The Russians had help from someone on the Norwegian side. Someone who knew where an excursion party of young women from the university was going to be."

"The police?"

"No. They're too dumb," said Jaske. "Maybe border guards, the army, or just a criminal gang on this side who wanted to do a human trafficking deal. We're not safe here just yet. The police can't protect us."

"There's someone this side of the border involved, someone powerful," Blackwood added.

"Where are the girls, though?"

"They're bussing them to Tromsø. They'll be safe there. That's why I made it so public."

"They won't do anything against Russia," Anda said. "It will all blow over."

Jaske went quiet and gazed at the dark road ahead.

They took a long, winding road that skirted a black lake, or maybe the sea, with just an occasional glimmer of light from a house set back from the road, but mostly just a bleak darkness with not a single vehicle coming the other way. This was the hinterland.

After forty minutes, Ande pulled into an unassuming gap in the stones that lined the road and vaulted a rocky path. The car juddered and rocked as it climbed. Lights came to view — lights you couldn't see from the road — and a floodlight switched on as they pulled up outside a red cottage. White reindeer hides nailed to the walls, splayed out, and bulbous kidney-red carcasses hung from the eaves, swaying in the breeze.

A grey-haired woman came out, arms open and Jaske ran to her, almost knocking her over. They wept and Anda joined them, hugging them both. The mother stroked her daughter's face, wiping her tears away.

Blackwood watched it, standing outside the pool of light, alone in the shadow, and had a dreadful realization. They might have escaped, but Curtis and Beria were only after him — and he'd brought them right to Jaske's home.

45

NOVEMBER 15TH, 1983. CREDENHILL, Hereford.

"At ease, private," the colonel said. "This is off the books."

There was that phrase again. Like there was ever anything that was 'on the books' in this place.

He let his torso slump, just a little, in the stiff wooden chair, but felt more conscious of his body.

The officer seemed to sense it with a wry smile. He rose and went to a cabinet behind him and poured whisky from a green bottle.

He could make out the name *Johnny Walker* but it wasn't a bottle he'd ever seen before.

He came back with two glasses and put one in his hand. The private stared at it like he'd handed him a lobster.

What was this?

On the wall behind the officer, two portraits: one of the Queen and another the Prime Minister, who gazed down on them with a steely smile, and maybe just the hint of a nod and a wink.

He took a gulp of the whisky. It burned his throat and he fought not to cough. But he felt his shoulders slacken. It would take the whole bottle before he could follow the command: *at ease.*

The officer sipped at his whisky ever so slightly, almost just breathing it in, hardly drinking it at all. That must be how you made a whisky last as long as a pint in the mess.

"There were a couple of details I wanted to go over, in your report." He tapped a card file on his desk but didn't open it.

"Sir?"

"There are a just a few details that don't fit with the narrative we have from our alternative sources."

Here it was: the cover up, the subtle pressure to print the lie. He took a sip of the whisky, just the slightest inhalation, and let it linger for a moment before swallowing. That was better. "I know what I saw, sir."

"Understandable, in all the confusion, that you might make such a mistake, but it was clearly a Russian fighter that attacked. Only to be expected. The Norwegians had accidentally crossed the border, and your patrol too."

Fuck it. This would be his last hurrah.

They were going to drum him out. It didn't matter anymore. He could say what he liked. "With respect, sir, we all know the Russians and Norwegians have an understanding. They accidentally cross the border, they get 72 hours to cross back to their side."

"Rather more complicated with a Pathfinder patrol doing the same. Which, of course, we can't shout about."

"It was a Yank fighter. I saw it. F-16."

"Human error. Entirely understandable. Nothing to be done about it."

"I'm not going to change my report, sir."

The officer didn't thump the table and shout and scream. He smiled again — that supercilious smile just like the PM's on the wall behind him — a smile that said your truth is immaterial. We make our own reality.

"What do you imagine happened?" the officer asked.

"A clusterfuck. That's what happened."

"But why would our American allies attack a rescue mission in this way. It doesn't make sense. We have a clear signal from SIS reporting the situation. It was clear to everyone on our side."

"The signal was changed."

"Why? To what end?"

And this is where he had him. There was no logic to it. None at all. "I don't know, sir."

The officer nodded. "Hmmm. I thought you might say that. There are, you see, some things that are beyond our rank, our pay grade, if you will. And in this case, we have to believe it was simply a matter of friendly fire. A mistake. Someone made a mistake. Though we can never say that, of course. And never suggest it on the record." He tapped the card file again.

"Friendly fire, my arse. Someone set us up."

The officer nodded. He took a slug of his whisky. Quick this time, like he wanted this over and done with.

"Sorry, sir. It's what I saw, sir."

"So I'm to approve a report that says there was a tremendous cock-up by our American cousins. The signal was changed. Somehow it went from a Brit team escorting Norwegian nationals back across the border, to Brits and Norwegians captured and a Spetsnaz team crossing onto Allied soil."

"They attacked us on the Russian side."

"They got lost. The border is a little, shall we say, fluid, over there, hmm?"

The private took a slug of whisky. Might as well finish it. This was going nowhere. It no longer burned. It was a blast of sea spume and hospital floors.

The officer gazed into his glass a little too long, lost in a private thought, and then he said, "What you *saw* is immaterial."

"So, you believe me?"

The colonel opened a box on his desk and took out a cigarette. Offered it.

The private shook his head.

The colonel lit his and puffed out smoke. "I'm afraid this is the world we live in now."

"Well, it bloody stinks, sir."

The colonel looked up again with something that seemed like pity. Then he smiled and nodded. "You've seen what it is. The Americans want to heat up the Cold War. Unfortunately, we were the kindling. And there's nothing we can do about it." He rapped his knuckles on the report. "This is the official history and this is what we say, should anyone ever ask about this again."

"Yes, sir."

"Your part in this has been exemplary. You avoided capture by the enemy, found your way back to safety across several hundred miles of hostile territory without being captured. That's worthy of the George Cross."

The Prime Minister winked down at him again. Was she laughing?

"But as the operation was so secret, I'm afraid you won't get a medal. But you will get a promotion. I'm proud to say you are Lieutenant now. For your extraordinary gallantry."

For keeping my mouth shut.

This time he knew he hadn't said it. There would be so many more times he would keep it to himself, keep all their rotten lies inside himself and say nothing.

The colonel rose and held out his hand to the new lieutenant. "Well done, Curtis." he said.

He shook the colonel's hand — it was cold and clammy — and he fought the desire to wipe his hand on his tunic.

He turned and marched out, leaving his commanding officer to his whisky with only Margaret Thatcher and the Queen for company.

The cold air met him and he paused under the clocktower. The balling of a sergeant somewhere. There was always a sergeant yelling.

He wiped his hand on his tunic and marched off, his face pounding like thunder, and something still burning in his throat. It wasn't the whisky. He had a feeling no amount of whisky in the world would remove the bad taste in his mouth.

46

THE MOTHER DRAGGED THEM inside the red hut to a comfortably cluttered interior, so hot that Blackwood felt the marrow in his bones thawing.

"This is my mother," Jaske said. "Her name is Seita."

Blackwood shook her hand and bowed. "I'm pleased to meet you, Seita."

Jaske gave her a long explanation about the Englishman who rescued her. Anda took his puffa jacket off and motioned Blackwood to the large wooden table that dominated the room. Smells drifted from the kitchen that made his belly growl.

Seita talked in Sámi and Anda murmured translations.

"I saw you on the internet in the square at Kirkenes. My heart leapt for joy. We've been hearing all the rumours on the internet. So many of them. Such awful things they have been saying."

Anda dug out his phone and scrolled through pages of text and pictures. "There are already thousands saying it's fake and you're a government agent."

Jaske laughed.

It was the first time Blackwood had seen her laugh.

Seita pointed at the phone and shouted at Anda. He said something back in Sámi and they appeared to be having an argument.

"She says I should tell our father that Jaske is back, but I tell her I already have. Only he won't have a signal where he is, so he won't get it. She doesn't understand that no matter how good the signal is here, it doesn't matter if he doesn't have a signal there."

Seita waved her hands dismissively and went to the kitchen. Jaske followed and they came back moments later with dishes for the table.

Blackwood got up. "Can I help?"

All three of them motioned him to sit.

"You're our guest," said Jaske.

"And a hero," said Anda. "Sit and be the hero."

Blackwood shrugged and sat back, aware of the two Makarov pistols digging into the small of his back, shoved into his jeans. He wondered if he should ask Jaske if there might be a place he could put them, but it seemed impolite to draw attention to his weaponry. And there was the nagging thought that he wanted them in easy reach if Curtis and his goons dropped by on a social visit. He mentally ticked off the bullets and tried to count how many left, the urge to take each pistol out and check the magazines gnawing at him.

Seita planted a plate piled high with flatbread in the middle of the table.

"Mmmmm, *gáhkko,*" Jaske purred. "I missed *gáhkko* so much." She took one, tore it and chewed it, swooning. "They fed us on Russian crap like borscht and cabbage."

They sat and tucked into the array of dishes.

"This is cloudberry jam," Jaske said. "Very good. You'll like it."

Blackwood smirked, not sure he had a choice. He spread some on the flatbread and chewed on it. It was divine, but anything would taste divine after what they'd been through. He couldn't remember when he'd last eaten something. Perhaps the thin soup Jaske had fed him. There hadn't even been any day with which to gauge what meals might be due.

Jaske spooned what looked like giant meatballs on his plate, with potatoes. The others spooned the cloudberry jam on theirs so Blackwood did the same.

"This is *gumppus,*" Jaske said. "You might be horrified. It's blood cakes."

"Hey, we have things like that in England too."

"Really?"

"Yeah, black pudding. That's like a blood sausage. I used to have it with every fried breakfast."

Blackwood bit into one. It was decent. Spicy and pungent. Not too much like black pudding, fresher, somehow, cleaner. "This is good food," he said. "Delicious."

Jaske translated it for her mother and she beamed with pride. He noted they ate one-handed because Seita wouldn't let go of Jaske's hand.

They talked some more in Sámi and the brother, Anda, didn't bother to translate. Blackwood finished his plate of food. They were wasting time. He couldn't be certain how long it would take them to track Jaske down.

At a pause in the conversation he said, "Is this your address, Jaske? Where you live, I mean, officially?"

"No. I'm based at Tromsø, near the university."

"That's good."

"Why?" Anda asked.

"Nothing. Just wondering."

"You think the police will come here?" Jaske asked.

"Maybe," Blackwood said. He was thinking more that it might be Curtis and the Russians.

"That settles it," Jaske said.

Blackwood looked from one to the other, waiting for an explanation.

"My father is out taking a pilgrimage to our *storjunkare*."

Anda snorted but said nothing.

"It's our place where we make a sacrifice and pray for good fortune. Just our family's place. Mother says the rock must have answered his prayers because here I am."

She caught Blackwood's befuddled look. "The *storjunkare* is a rock out there in the wilds. It's a spirit rock that belongs to our family. We visit it every year and give sacrifice to it."

"Sacrifice?"

"Yes, usually a virgin girl from the village."

He caught her blank face, shocked for a moment, then cracked a smile.

She grinned. She'd got him good and proper.

"We spread twigs under them in winter, in a nice pattern, and leaves in summer. My father likes to give a reindeer steak."

"I see."

"I suppose you think it's simple and stupid."

He shook his head. "No. Why would I?"

She shrugged and looked away, blushing. That flush in her cheeks when she was angry. "I have to go to him."

Blackwood nodded, pushing his plate away. "Then I have to go with you."

Anda got up and disappeared to the other room. Seita cleared the plates.

"You don't," Jaske said. "You've done enough."

"I'm sort of responsible for you now."

"You aren't."

He felt the pull of... home, was it? Did he have anything he could call home? His daughter whom he didn't know and had only seen for a couple of days — the weekend of a killing spree — it was hardly daddy-daughter stuff. She was, he hoped, in London now, with her mother and a car full of banknotes. That was the plan. The most fucked up family reunion on earth. That was all he could offer. The best he could do. Because at the end of the day, he was just a guy who'd been trained to kill people, destroy things, brutalized by the army, then by a gang of criminals, then by prison. He was best out of his daughter's life forever. A car boot full of blood money was all he was good for.

"I know I'm not responsible for you," he said. "But I'd like to help you do this. Sort of see you home safely."

"You're walking me to my door?" There was that grin again. Better than the flush of anger.

"Yes. If you like."

"But we haven't even been on a date."

"Sorry. I'm not much of a traditional guy."

Her smile dropped. He'd said it with too much of a thread of maudlin self-pity. Look at me — what I've become. I'm not fit to live among the humans.

"Okay," she said. "Take me home."

Anda returned and paused, with the sense of someone who knows they're interrupting.

Jaske got up and went to the kitchen, giving a stream of instructions to her mother. They rushed to another room, chattering.

Anda stared across the table. "We're all going to our *storjunkare?*"

Jaske had introduced him as her older brother, but he seemed much younger, a scared boy. Jaske was so much more a fighter. But then perhaps the last few weeks had turned her into that fighter. It was clear that Jaske was more than capable of fighting back, but Anda and the mother would be a serious tactical weak spot.

Blackwood shook his head. "You need to get out of here and take your mother somewhere safe."

"Why?"

"The police will want to talk to Jaske after she ran out on them. They'll come here eventually."

"You said you didn't think the police would be a problem."

"I think the police don't have the best security. Anyone could hack into that and beat them to it. Is there some place you can go where no one knows you? Some place where the authorities won't know to come looking for Jaske?"

Anda put his phone on the table. He seemed frozen, having to process it all. Too slow. Too slow to survive.

Jaske returned and stood in the doorway, sensing she was interrupting something this time. Her mother came to her side and held her.

"The men who took your sister. They're a criminal gang with very big connections to the military. The Russian and Norwegian military. They are ruthless and they're looking for me. I have information they want."

"Then leave us," Anda said.

"I'd happily do that. But I know they're going to come looking for Jaske, and that means they're coming here. They will kill you, whether you tell them where I am or not. They will kill both of you."

Anda fondled his phone and swallowed.

"The only thing I can do is get her away."

"And what then?"

"I lure them in and kill them all."

"The Russian and Norwegian army?" Anda scoffed. "You're going to kill them all?"

"He can do it," Jaske said. "Believe me."

She gave her brother a stream of Sámi. Anda and Seita listened with growing horror. Blackwood recognized only one word.

The Norwegian had rolled and bucked under him, a pig at slaughter, kicking and squealing. He'd choked and growled a single word.

"Jaevel."

His eyes bulging with terror. His legs kicking and banging the floor.

And then he kicked a little less.

And then he didn't move at all.

And then he was dead.

"I have a friend," Anda said. "He has a hunting lodge. We can go there."

"Don't call him. Just turn up and ask him. And make sure he tells no one."

Anda nodded. It was settled. He explained it all to his mother while Jaske took Blackwood to a back room where she tossed him a snowsuit. It was light material, the kind of modern, hi-tech clothing skiers wore. It went over his clothes neatly and it was like sitting before a roaring fire. He carefully removed one of the Makarovs to the jacket pocket.

"You take this one," he said, tossing the other gun to her.

She put it in her pocket. Hers was more of an indigo smock with a red plaid shawl pinned tight around her shoulders and a matching red bonnet.

They came out to find Anda and Seita ready to leave. The mother hugged her daughter and fought back tears. They embraced and talked in Sámi before Anda pulled her away and put her in the car.

Jaske and Blackwood watched them drive off into the darkness.

"How are we travelling?" Blackwood asked.

"Come and see," she said.

She took him round the back of the hut, the motion-detector lamps lighting their way, to a shed. She pulled a tarpaulin aside to reveal a snowmobile.

"Cool," he said.

She busied herself checking the fuel.

"That Norwegian we killed," Blackwood said. "The one who was going to rape you."

"Orvik."

"That was his name?"

"Yes."

Orvik. Another name to add to the long roll call of death at his hands. Half the people on the list did not even have names. "He said something just before he died. What was it? *Jaevel* or something?"

"It was *Devil*. He called you *Devil.*"

Blackwood mulled it over. A dying man delivering his last word. He had looked right into Blackwood's soul and spat it in his face. Blackwood nodded and shrugged. "I suppose it's better than *Shitboot.*"

Jaske got on the snowmobile and Blackwood sat behind her.

"Hold on tight," she said.

She let the throttle out and with a great vibrating roar, they lurched away and skimmed out over the vast darkness.

47

SEITA GOT IN THE car with her son and put the seatbelt on. Cold air blasted from the dashboard and the footwell before it warmed up after a minute. Normally, Anda would leave the engine running a little to warm the car up before they got in, but this was an emergency and so it was all such a rush to leave the house.

Her daughter only home an hour and already they were split up.

Anda eased the car over the bumpy, rocky pathway and down to the road where it gripped the gritted tarmac, and the engine roared with bravado as he struggled up the road towards Kirkenes. How much longer did this clapped-out piece of junk have left to live, she wondered, and then her son would need money, always money. His sister's return had only marked again the contrast between the life she'd made for herself and the life Anda hadn't. She had smothered him. Guhtur had taken Jaske and turned her into a boy while she had kept their son tied to her apron. It was always the way.

Anda tapped the steering wheel, drumming an agitated rhythm, and muttered something under his breath and punched the wheel.

"What was that, Anda?" she asked.

"Oh? Nothing."

He hadn't realized he was talking to himself, arguing with himself, cursing at some thought. The world always railing at Anda in his head.

She patted his thigh and peered at the dark road ahead, ignoring his puzzled glance.

They were only two minutes along the coast road when a border police car confronted them. A big black SUV. They flashed the blue light and an arm came out of the window to wave them down.

"What the hell?" Anda groaned.

Men in black jumped out and one of them pointedly stood in front so they couldn't drive off, a machine gun across his belly.

The police chief who was on the television earlier. Eriksen was his name. He had looked like a blundering fool, trying to pretend he'd rescued the missing girls all by himself, and losing one of them before he'd finished his speech.

He signalled Anda to step out of the car. Anda unhooked his seatbelt and stepped out to the cold, slamming the door behind. They talked in muffled Norwegian.

Seita stepped out and came round.

"Mother, get back inside," Anda said.

"What's going on, officer?" she asked.

They spoke in Norwegian, not Sámi. This was the way it was. You couldn't say anything in your own language in case the police thought you were talking in secret. So you had to speak Norwegian. You had to speak the coloniser's language in your own land.

"What is this?" she asked. "Why are you stopping us?"

"Madam, I'm afraid your daughter left too soon. We need to question her some more."

"So she escapes a kidnapping and now she's a suspect?"

"She has vital information if we're going to bring the kidnappers to justice."

"She's gone to father's *storjunkare*," Anda said, pointing a flailing hand back down the road. "And I need to take my mother somewhere safe."

Eriksen wavered, looked at his underlings, like a man who wasn't sure he was in charge. "I need you to take me to your sister right now."

"Please, man, I'm begging you," Anda pleaded. "Let me take my mother. It's just an hour away."

Eriksen glanced over his shoulder. "I can't."

Now she looked at it, one of the men was not in a border police uniform, but black paramilitary with no markings. And his face.

"Who is this?" she asked.

"He's helping us."

"He looks Russian."

"We needed a Russian tracker to help us find the missing girls," Eriksen said. "And his race isn't an issue."

"I didn't say anything about his race."

"I won't have our neighbours subjected to this racism."

Seita snorted a laugh. "You want to talk about racism, we can sit down and I'll tell you some stories."

"There's no need for all of this. I'm taking your son and if you want, I'll take you too."

"No!" Anda yelled.

Another pang of concern flared in her breast. So touching that he wanted to shield his mother from this —

a mother who would tear these men's hearts out to protect her children.

"Let me take my mother to my cousin. It's just an hour."

"I can't do that," Eriksen said.

Seita patted her son's arm. "Anda. You go with the police. If they need to talk to Jaske, you ought to take them to her."

"But I'm supposed to take you—"

"I'm okay. I can drive myself back home. I'll wait for you there."

The Russian scout barked something in his native tongue, all oily and squirming, like an eel you couldn't nail down.

Eriksen seemed to understand. Of course, a border guard out here would have to speak Russian too. But this was strange. It was almost like the scout was the boss.

Eriksen went red in the face and barked back. He was standing his ground. Good for him. These Russians were taking over. They came over the border every day to shop and now there were even Russian street signs for them. Before you knew it, this place would be Russian. That's what the Norwegians said. She had always laughed at that. This was the Sápmi. Norwegians, Russians, Finns, Swedes, it didn't matter: they all fought over whose land this was, while the Sámi stood here rooted to the earth.

She moved to open the car door to get in the driver's seat.

Eriksen placed his hand on his firearm. "Can you call your husband and let him know we're coming?"

"Pah!" She scoffed and waved a dismissive hand. "There's no signal where he is. And I don't have a phone either. Horrible things."

Anda nodded to confirm this.

"Okay," said Eriksen. "She can go back home."

There was something about his face. He'd been embarrassed on the television. Everyone had seen him bumbling his way through an impromptu press conference in the street, cameras and lights pushed into his fat face. He had looked surprised, like he didn't know what to do with Jaske and the girls — like a model had landed in his lap. A big, overgrown boy pretending to be a sheriff, hardly away from his mother's teat, the milk still on his lips. These poor boys who couldn't become men. Like her son. Trying so hard to be a man. His sister out there at the *storjunkare* with their father, being the son he needed. Wasn't it always the way?

Eriksen barked something in Russian to the scout.

Anda placed the keys in her palm and squeezed her hand. Eriksen pulled him away to the SUV.

As they took him away, her eyes met her son's and a pang of concern flared in her breast. Her son taken by the police. He had embarrassed this man when he'd rescued his sister. But he had done it from the goodness in his heart. Every brother in the world would do the same. He wasn't a criminal. But that didn't always matter out here.

They got in the SUV and roared off up the coast road.

She got in the car and turned the ignition. Reversed to the overtaking bay twenty yards back and did a quick three-point turn to head back to the house.

Before she turned into the stone driveway, she dug her mobile out of her pocket and keyed up her husband's number. If the police were coming, it was always best to know in advance, no matter how much they said they were coming to help. It was always the way.

48

BLACKWOOD HELD ON TIGHT, his arms around Jaske's waist. As much as he could, in the darkness, he sensed they were travelling south-east, almost heading back to the Russian border they'd crossed earlier that day.

Was it today? he wondered. There really was no day. There was nothing but the night. There was no horizon, just a grey moonlit void. It was dizzying.

The snowmobile's headlight swept the snow before them, revealing twenty yards of crisp white plain, occasionally the fringe of a forest, dark trees standing sentinel.

At one point, pinprick lights danced in the dark before them. A swathe of them, like it was a road in the distance or a string of lanterns. Dark shapes formed behind the lights and all at once he realized it was a herd of reindeer. They bolted and scattered into the night.

After about forty minutes, she pulled up and killed the engine and headlights. A sudden awesome silence.

"How the hell do you know where to go in this blackness? It's like you have a GPS system in your soul."

She smiled. "I've been doing it all my life. I could do it with a blindfold."

Blackwood's eyes adjusted to the dark, the moonlight illuminating a great clearing where a rock formation sheltered a couple of dark triangular shapes, a glow inside each.

"Wigwams?" he said.

"They're called *lavvu,*" Jaske corrected him.

A figure emerged from one of them and stood silently watching. A man. The telltale shape of a rifle in hand.

"*Áhttje!*" Jaske called.

"Jaske?" the man said. An old voice, cracked and gnarled like aged wood. He slung the rifle on his shoulder.

She ran to his embrace and they chattered in Sámi. Blackwood gave it a minute and then headed towards them, trudging through the snow.

Jaske switched to English. "*Áhttje,* this is Blackwood. He's English. He helped me escape."

The old man came and clasped Blackwood's outstretched hand, clasping it in both of his and shaking it warmly. He had a white beard and piercing blue eyes.

"Welcome," he said. "My name is Guhtur. Come inside."

They followed him through the flap. Reindeer hide, Blackwood noted. Inside it was spacious, a campfire in the centre and more reindeer hides scattered over straw. A flush of warmth.

"I pitched two *lavvu*," the old man said, standing his rifle in the corner. "Because I knew you would come. The gods would make it happen if I prayed hard enough."

"You've lit a fire in mine."

"Of course. So you come home to a warm *lavvu*." He looked to Blackwood and added, "If it's minus thirty outside it's the same inside, if there's no fire."

Jaske sat beside her father, her hand on his knee. Blackwood sat across the fire. Guhtur fussed with a pot that hung over the smouldering logs and poured coffee into tin cups.

It was bitter and strong and warm and perfect. Blackwood breathed it in and hummed.

"And you wore your *gákti*. This is good. You are truly home."

Blackwood wondered if Jaske had always worn traditional clothes at home, or if it had been a point of dispute between them.

Jaske lapsed into her native language, but it was clear she was relating what had happened. She pointed to Blackwood a few times, and Guhtur stroked his beard and nodded. Blackwood feared she was relating what an efficient killer he was. She pointed to his shoulder and said, "Show him."

Blackwood pulled his fleece and shirt aside to reveal his wound.

The old man examined it and smiled. "Your *duodji* is not so good."

"*Duodji* is Sámi craft," Jaske explained. "Needlework. I wasn't in the best mood to make it perfect. I'm sorry."

Blackwood pulled his clothes back down and shrugged. He couldn't blame her. He'd just been another man, another killer, for all she knew.

"So, you rescue my daughter and return her home," Guhtur said. "For this I am forever in your debt."

"She didn't need my help," Blackwood said. "She did it all herself. In a way, she rescued me."

Guhtur slapped his daughter's thigh. "I raise this one to be tough, to fight. She is more of a fighter than her brother."

Jaske winced at her father's laughter.

"I expected the border to be more... fortified," Blackwood said.

"Stalin wanted an electrified fence across the Finnmárku," Guhtur said. "The problem was one of power. How do you electrify a 75-mile border? They ignored the climate, wildlife and human inhabitants."

"Why not build a barbed wire fence; no electricity?" Blackwood asked.

"The permafrost. It spits out anything you concrete in. Within a month your fences fall over. And the reindeer. Five hundred deer won't be stopped by a fence. They go straight through."

Jaske pointed to the south-west. "We're very close to the border again, but north of where we crossed it."

Blackwood smiled to himself. He'd sensed it too. Maybe he had the same GPS in his soul.

"If you go straight that way, you reach Linhammar. Only about twelve kilometres."

A strange feeling of *déjà vu* about this whole conversation. *Linhammar*. There it was again. Where did he know that from?

Curtis.

"What's at *Linhammar?*"

Jaske shrugged. "A harbour. A military base. There's a diving centre for tourists, I think, as well."

"So it's not all a military base?"

"I think parts of it used to be a military base that became a ghost town, so now there's a tourist part for divers, and there's a military museum as well. But the harbour is military. Mostly border patrol boats. Why?"

"Curtis used to talk about it. Something important."

"What happened?" she asked.

"Something bad," Blackwood said. "I don't know what. But he talked about it, rambling, drunk. Something scarred him. He was always bitter, always told his men that the top brass might screw them over and never to trust their commanding officers."

"That doesn't sound like a good unit commander."

"It made sense. He created a camaraderie in the team. They'd do anything for each other. It was always them against the world, including our own side. You ended up worshipping your leader."

"And did you worship him?"

Blackwood shrugged and avoided her gaze. "Maybe. A little. Until I stepped out of line. I questioned him. And when you question him, you question the team. They came for me."

"A plane was shot down there," Guhtur said. He stroked his white beard. "A Norwegian plane shot down. During a training exercise. There were Americans and British troops here. NATO. It was like that in the Cold War. I don't know much about it. Some kind of cover up. Old Viggu knows it." He pointed out south. "He was there. He was a scout for the army."

Blackwood tried to remember through the fog of some drunken night in the mess, years ago. A plane going down. Curtis had talked about it. But there was only that word: *Linhammar*.

"Those were bad times," Guhtur said. He poked the fire with a stick. "I fear those times are here again."

Without warning, he sang. A pulsing refrain with a simple modulation. Almost like yodelling, but deeper, sadder. His croaking voice hit high notes and cracked.

When he finished, Blackwood wondered if he should clap.

"That was a *joik*," Jaske said. "It's a song we sing about a person or a place. My father sang his usual *joik* about me but also changed it to give thanks for my return."

"It was very nice," Blackwood said.

Jaske didn't answer or look at him. She sang.

Her *joik* was more dissonant, minor key. She sang it to the fire. A haunting refrain that hung over the crackling logs and rose with the smoke.

She finished, and they both looked at him. Blackwood had the uncomfortable feeling they might want him to sing too. He only knew some dirty rugby songs from the mess.

"A *joik* is also like a courting ritual," Guhtur said with a smile. "It's always dedicated to a single thing or person and the harmonies attempt to capture the person."

Jaske stared into the flames and wouldn't look up at him.

"That one sounded like a dark place," Blackwood said.

The old man grunted agreement. "I've never heard one that dark. They don't usually mention *Ruohtta*."

"*Áhttje,*" Jaske said, admonishing him.

"What? It was his *joik*. He should know it."

"What's roo-ot-ta?" Blackwood asked.

Jaske shook her head. "It doesn't matter."

She gave her father a stream of Sámi and they talked. Blackwood sensed the subject had changed and her father was now asking her an important question. A slightly embarrassing conversation. Guhtur glanced at Blackwood as Jaske talked.

They were debating something to do with him. He tried not to feel embarrassed.

Jaske was insistent on something. Finally, she kissed her father and got up.

"Come," she said to Blackwood. "We're sleeping in my *lavvu.*"

Blackwood nodded, cast a glance at the rifle sitting behind Guhtur, and said *goodnight.*

49

THE FIRE IN THE other *lavvu* was low, embers smouldering crimson. Jaske poked them with a stick and loaded a couple of logs. The fire took and licked into flame again, crackling and roaring.

Blackwood sat on a pile of reindeer hide he assumed was his bed for the night, and Jaske lay on hers across from him.

"We Sámi are always stuck in the middle," Jaske said, "unrecognized by both sides because we have no respect for their border."

She had taken it up again as if they were still sitting with her father in the *lavvu* next door; still having the same conversation.

"They draw invisible lines on the land and say this is theirs. Four countries claim our land, but this is still the *Sápmi*." She saw Blackwood's frown. "Our nation is the

Sápmi and this part of the nation, this region here, is the *Finnmárku.*"

"Don't they call this place Lapland?" Blackwood asked.

Jaske snorted. "They call it Lapland to market their Santa Claus holidays. But this is the *Sápmi* and we are the *Sámi olbmot.* The people of the *Sápmi.* The *Sápmi* is both the Sámi land and the Sámi people. We are this land, and this land is us."

Blackwood wondered if this had been her cultural talk to the Norwegian student girls, just before they'd been kidnapped. She was reciting it as if she needed to anchor herself to home.

"Norway, Finland, Sweden and Russia all claim these lands," she said, bitterly, "and the Russians have their militarised zone, but we Sámi hold this place. We're not Russian or Finnish. We're not Norwegian or Swedish."

They lay silent, with just the crackling of the fire, and Blackwood gazed at the pinnacle of the lavvu, where the poles crossed and smoke crept out to the stars. After a while he said, "What's *roo-ot-ta?*"

She didn't want to answer.

"Your father said it, after you sang the song."

"He's one of our spirits."

"Your father said the song was about me, but he'd never heard one that mentioned this *roo-ot-ta.*"

"*Ruohtta* rules the underworld."

"So he's like a god..."

"Yes."

"The god of the underworld."

"Yes."

"Isn't that like the devil?"

"He's the god of Death," she said.

Like Orvik had hissed as Blackwood had strangled the last drop of life out of him.

Jaevel. The devil.

That was what he was. The stench of death was all over him, in his clothes, his hair, his skin. It had seeped through to his bones. Or maybe it had been inside all the time and the smell was seeping outward.

"If you don't live according to the natural orders," Jaske said, "you go to *Rotaimo*, the underground. And *Ruohtta* rules there. Once you are there, you get a new body, but you can never leave *Rotaimo*."

He stared into the fire for a long time.

"Blackwood?" she said.

"Yes?"

"Come into my bed."

50

SHE WAS NAKED UNDER the reindeer hide. He hadn't noticed her undress. Before he'd pressed against her, she was tearing off his t-shirt and pants, making him as naked as her.

He flinched as he pressed against her, the wound burning. She stroked the stitching, gently. He let out a gasp of pain. It hurt like hell.

"I'm sorry," she whispered. "I wish I'd done a better job of this."

She went away from his lips and shuddered down his body till her face was at his navel. He thought she was going to take him in her mouth, but she kissed the wound, her lips nudging the hard crust of the stitching.

She came back up and straddled him, sitting above him, throwing back the reindeer hide. The firelight flickered all over her skin, golden brown. Reaching down between her legs, she guided him inside her and he felt the close, secret warmth of her taking him, consuming him.

She moaned a lullaby. A low *joik* for him, or for this place, or for this act.

His hands reached up for her breasts and he took the mysterious weight of them in his palms, her nipples thickening to his touch.

Her low throat song erupted in a shriek and she snapped a hand to her mouth, grinning shyly.

He put his fingers in her mouth and she sucked on them and rubbed harder against him, her hips pulsing, biting his hand as she ground her pleasure.

"What's that?" she gasped.

They stopped, both holding their breath.

An engine. The low drone of an engine approaching through the night.

Jaske leapt up and tussled with her clothes.

Not one engine. Two. Roaring towards them.

Blackwood fumbled for his clothes, pulling on his boots. He thought for a moment they might ride on right through them, but the engines came to a halt.

He reached for his Makarov and so did Jaske.

Too late.

Car doors slammed. Boots trudged in the snow.

"Blackwood!" Curtis's voice rent the still night air. "Come out, or we machine gun the shit out of you in there."

Blackwood and Jaske stood frozen and he remembered getting caught sleeping with a girlfriend when he was a kid. The same fumble for clothes and the frantic shame of being caught with his trousers down, wanting to make sure he was dressed enough for the fight with the angry father. Just as then, there was no escape, and half his anger was at allowing himself to get caught.

He let the Makarov drop and pinched the handle between his thumb and forefinger.

Jaske did the same.

There was no shooting their way out of this.

51

HE STEPPED OUT FIRST, blinded by headlights, hands up, holding the gun far aside. Jaske stepped out after him.

"Drop the weapons," Curtis called.

Two jeeps were parked up twelve feet apart to approach wide on two fronts. A cluster of heads behind the lights. Maybe eight men. It would be Curtis and Beria, and each with two or three goons to back them up: all the men they hadn't managed to shoot off that long road from Vayda-Guba. Those headlights that had followed them quietly all the way.

Blackwood and Jaske both dropped their pistols into the snow.

"Who's in the other tent?"

"It's empty," Jaske called, her voice thick with despair.

Curtis signalled some of the men to go look. They crept close. One of them lifted the flap and pointed his machine gun inside.

Blackwood expected the old man to shoot him in the face, but nothing happened. The soldier peered inside. The old man didn't call out surrender and come out with his hands up.

The goon with the machine gun shook his head.

Guhtur had gone. This was good. Perhaps he was out there. Perhaps he had his rifle.

"Why two tents?" Curtis asked, as if amused at a private joke.

"It's his," Jaske said. "He came to mine in the night."

Curtis laughed a sinister, cynical little laugh. "Blackwood. You dirty dog. Sampling the wares." Then his grin dropped. "Where's your father?"

Beria barked out orders in a crackle of Russian. Two the men turned away and covered the surrounding land.

Blackwood wondered how they knew Jaske's father was out there, armed, and how they'd come right to this spot. Did he have a tracker on him — something in his clothes — perhaps in his boot — something they might have placed in there when he was unconscious just in case he ran for it? Might they have placed it there right from the start and that was how Beria had known which way he'd go? That was how they'd followed so easily, a mile behind, all the way from Vayda-Guba to this very spot.

The drone of an engine out there somewhere, nearing.

Jaske whimpered. Her father returning. He would blunder right here into this trap, and he was the only hope they had of getting out of this.

Distant pinpricks of light. A jeep of some kind. The two goons who had their guns trained on it fanned out to hit it from each side if need be.

As it neared, Blackwood looked for the telltale sign of a white beard but he couldn't make out who was at the wheel. He hadn't seen Guhtur's vehicle, but this was a field wagon, dark, maybe black.

"That your father's car?" he murmured.

"No," Jaske said.

No, a siren on top.

"Ooh," said Curtis, "looks like the cavalry are here."

Curtis laughed and Blackwood had the horrible thought that the police were going to blunder into a bloodbath.

"Border police," Jaske said, puzzled.

They allowed the SUV to come to a stop. No one shot. The engine died and four figures stepped out: three men in uniform and a fourth in civilian attire.

It was the policeman who'd greeted the bus in Kirkenes. And the civilian who stepped out with them was...

"Anda?" Jaske said.

"I said I'd bring them here if they didn't harm you or father," Anda replied.

"You brought them to us?"

He wasn't handcuffed, Blackwood noticed. Something in the way he held himself, in the way none of the Russians were concerned. They knew these men; they'd worked with them before. This cop had been working with Curtis and the Russians all along, and Anda...

"You fucking traitor!" Jaske screamed.

She ran at her brother. The goons raised their guns. Beria shouted something with disdainful indifference.

Jaske slammed into her brother, punching and kicking. He cowered and yelled out something in Sámi.

Curtis said, "Eriksen, you're here to maintain law and order."

The cop sighed and yanked Jaske away, throwing her so she fell in the snow. She leaped up again, growling defiance. Eriksen punched her back down.

Blackwood flinched and stepped forward. Just one step. But there were six or more guns trained on him.

Eriksen kicked Jaske in the guts and snarled, *"Sámifitte!"*

She moaned and retched, coughing into snow.

The cop wiped the thread of drool from his mouth and circled back to the headlight glow.

"You said she'd be safe!" Anda yelled.

Eriksen smacked him across the face and Anda fell, howling, holding his nose.

Blackwood's fists balled. He'd seen this too many times: the low-ranking bully giving it out in a desperate attempt to assert power over someone, anyone, because he was someone else's bitch. This man, this cop, belonged to Curtis and Beria. And all at once he realized it now: he was the Norwegian contact who'd set up the kidnapping of Jaske and the student girls. A Norwegian cop who'd betrayed his own for a cut of the profits.

And her brother too.

"I always love to see a family reunion like this," Curtis scoffed. "Especially when it becomes clear exactly what family means."

"Why?" Jaske yelled.

"A police chief's salary isn't enough to live on," Curtis said. "Not out here in this godforsaken shithole."

But Jaske was looking at her brother.

"I was sick of it!" Anda screamed. "Sick of all this shit. Sick of being given the scraps. I wanted more — not just the sable legs for the Sámi people to turn into shitty hats."

Eriksen came for Jaske again, fists bared. "That's right, bitch. Guess who suggested an excursion of Norwegian students girls might be a good target."

"I didn't mean for you to be taken, though," Anda cried. "They told me they'd leave you! Trust me."

Jaske backed away, backward crawling.

The cop kicked at her feet.

"Leave her the fuck alone," Blackwood said, "or I'll tear your fucking arms off."

Eriksen rounded on Blackwood, spittle frothing at the corners of his mouth, insane with rage. But he held back, impotent, scared to take on this man who didn't fear him, even with a machine-gun-toting gang behind him.

Blackwood grinned, inviting him on.

"Enough!" Curtis shouted. "Bla Vesken, back in your kennel."

Eriksen spat and retreated, all bravado, glaring hate at Jaske still cowering in the snow.

Beria barked orders in Russian and his soldiers ran to Jaske and Anda and zip-tied their hands behind their backs.

Curtis marched through, pointing his pistol at Blackwood. "I'm going to give our Englishman one last chance to tell me what we need to know, and you're all going to keep quiet."

Curtis motioned him to the *lavvu* and Blackwood reluctantly stepped inside. As he crouched into the lavvu, his eyes met Jaske's, bent over the hood of the Hunter jeep, and he wondered if it was the last he'd see of her.

52

CURTIS SAT FACING THE door and motioned Blackwood to sit opposite, across the fire, back to the door. Basic psychology beloved of every shitty middle-manager who thought he was a magnate: having your back to the door made you vulnerable.

Blackwood sat down with a bump, hands tied behind his back, a flare of pain through his core. The knife. He still had the knife in his boot. He could throw it between Curtis's eyes. If only he could find a way to get his hands in front.

Curtis let his pistol lie flat on his knee. His finger still resting against the trigger guard, ready to shoot if Blackwood made any movement across the fire. It was too much to sit up and launch himself across the flames. He'd be dead before he got off his arse.

Maybe a kick. Kick the gun aside and boot him in the face.

But no. Curtis had seated himself well out of range.

"So what now? You going to carry on with your tedious torture routine and get it out of me?"

"Every man cracks in the end. Everyone gives up their secret when they're sitting in their own shit and blood."

"How's that going so far?"

Curtis shrugged, as if to concede the point. "So much fuss over a little bit of money," Curtis said.

"And a few women's lives. Remember them?"

"You don't care about them anymore than I do, Blackwood."

"That's where we're different."

Curtis chuckled, so sure he was looking at his disciple, a protege he'd moulded in his own image.

"One of them is dead, by the way."

"Yeah, I heard it on the news. When they find that Russian bullet in her, there might be an international incident."

He laughed, like it was all a joke. A trickster wreaking havoc at the border, causing a war, and cackling at the chaos he wrought.

"You're a fucking psychopath, Curtis. You must know that, right?"

"Talking of psychopaths, how *is* Brand?"

A qualm of suspicion crawled up Blackwood's spine. "What do you know about Brand?"

"More than you think. We go back a long, long way."

Blackwood scrambled to fill in the blanks: the whole Macduff operation that had been his own idea, then taken over by Brand, and somehow, at the end of it all, was Curtis. Too many strands all tangled up. Too many tentacles slithering, gripping, choking.

"He's dead," said Blackwood. "I killed him."

"I guess he had it coming."

"What do you know about that?"

A malicious smile. He was enjoying this: the thought that he knew more than you, that he had one over on you; like all good sociopaths.

"You think that ape was capable of fitting you up like he did?" Curtis snarled. "He couldn't plan a fucking corner shop robbery. To fuck someone's life up totally, to cut them loose from society, send them hurtling down into the depths of Hell — that takes someone who can see the long game. Someone who can plot a checkmate fifty moves ahead."

Blackwood's mind raced. He gasped, realizing he was hyperventilating.

It was Curtis who'd framed him.

Curtis laughed at the horror written on Blackwood's face. "Yes, I was the one who found your girl. I put you in prison. And in prison, I arranged those shivs. I might have known you'd be too much for a few amateur knife merchants."

"Why?"

"Oh, look at his sad little face. Clocktower, Blackwood. You don't walk out on that and think you can be a fucking bouncer on a nightclub door. You get fucked. You get erased."

"My daughter."

"That was unnecessary, I admit. I will give Brand the credit for that. Not my idea. But he's a psychopath, so what can you do? *Was* a psychopath."

"You arranged that mug who attacked me on the door too, didn't you?"

"A little teardrop to set off a tsunami."

"You think Brand's the psycho. You're..."

"What, Blackwood? A soldier? An assassin? A man who kills and bombs and mutilates because some politician tells him to? The things we did because we were ordered to. You did them too. Brand's nothing to what we are. If he's a psychopath, there's no word invented yet for what we are."

"Don't include me in this, you sick bastard."

"You're the same as me, Blackwood. You're up to your neck in blood too. You're wading through it just like I am. I can see the beauty of it, though. You will too."

Blackwood shook his head and chuckled at the dying embers. "Listen to yourself. You're gone."

"Join me, Blackwood. Together we can tear it all down and toast a Scotch on the rubble."

Join him in what? What rubble? What was he up to? There was something else going on that was nothing to do with Jaske, the women, the money, the whole shitty operation of greedy men pursuing dollars and stomping on everyone in their way.

"What are you doing here, Curtis? It's not the money, is it? What fuck up are you planning?"

"Oh, it's the money all right. Ten million is not something I'd give up on if I can find out where she is. You can do an awful lot with that kind of cash, and you pretty much dropped it into my lap."

He was trying to bring it back to that — the botched smuggling catastrophe — but it wasn't that at all.

"You'll never get your hands on it."

He tried to read Curtis's face. There was no concern at all about that fact.

Curtis said, "I always get what I want, Blackwood. You know that."

But he couldn't fake it. The money was not important to him. It was a side issue. It was an error in the quartermaster's accounts when this general was launching his final battle.

"There's something else," Blackwood said. "Something that doesn't include Beria. Something to do with Linhammar."

A flicker of concern crossed behind Curtis's eyes, like a burglar flitting past a bedroom window. He looked at the fire to hide it.

"Yeah," said Blackwood. "There it is. The truth at last."

Curtis looked up, hiding a grin, caught out, curious. "You remember Linhammar?"

"You used to rage about it every time you got drunk in the mess."

"Huh. I'm glad I got through to some of you."

"What happened at Linhammar?"

"I can't have raged that much, if you don't know."

"I was drunk too. Can't remember, mainly because I didn't give a fuck and it was irrelevant."

Anger flared, two bright livid flushes of crimson on his cheeks. "That's your problem, Blackwood. You were never that cut out for officer material."

"Yeah, I know. Couldn't kiss your arse enough. Too much thinking for myself."

Curtis closed his eyes and took in a long, deep breath. He let it out in a cloud of vapour. Like he'd gone to his special place, trying hard to control himself. Like if he hadn't, he'd have taken out his gun and put a bullet through Blackwood's forehead.

Finally, he opened his eyes and smirked, the wave of psychotic rage gone, blown out and dissipated in the cold air. "Have you seen the Northern Lights up here?"

Blackwood shook his head.

"They're quite a sight. There's going to be a particularly brilliant display tonight. Pity you won't see it?"

"And why won't I see it?"

"Because I'm going to take you outside and shoot you."

"But then you'll never know where the money is."

Curtis scoffed. "I've wasted enough time on you. There are more important manoeuvres to be getting on with."

What was this? He needed to know where the money was. Why would he kill Blackwood if he didn't have that information? What was more important than the money?

Curtis got up, his knees creaking, betraying his age. "Out."

Blackwood struggled to push himself up, his hands tied behind his back.

Curtis gave him the shove in the back he needed to propel himself through the door. He fell face first into the snow outside. Curtis yanked him up by the collar and threw him towards the jeeps.

Too many guns trained on them. No way out. And this was the end.

Curtis didn't care about the money, so there was no reason to keep Blackwood alive. For the first time, Blackwood had no hope left to cling to. He was going to die in the snow with a bullet through his head.

"He won't give us the information!" Curtis called. "So we're going to kill them all right here."

He felt the gun barrel press into the back of his head and peered through the headlights, looking for Jaske. At least let her be the last thing he saw.

Instead, he saw only Eriksen. The corrupt cop swallowed with the fear of a man who wasn't sure he would survive this.

Then his head exploded like a watermelon.

A gunshot echoed.

Eriksen crumpled and stained the snow, blood spraying a halo from the giant hole in his head.

Then the air was alive with gunfire.

53

ANOTHER SHOT ECHOED ACROSS the snowy plain. Another cop fell. Blackwood thought he caught a muzzle flash out to the west. A high calibre hunting rifle.

"Down!" he shouted.

Jaske hit the floor.

The Russians scattered. One of them fell into the pool of light. The others rushed for cover, shouting, calling, yelling their panic.

Curtis was gone. Blackwood tried to find him in the chaos. There, crouch sprinting for the jeeps.

Blackwood ducked and ran to the dead Russian, hot pain burning his thighs. A bullet whizzed past his face. He jerked and fell, ice smacking his cheek.

The Russians returned machine gun fire back at the darkness.

Blackwood sat up and struggled to inch himself to the dead Russian, pushing himself backward on his arse. His fumbling fingers caught the knife at the dead Russian's belt. He eased it from the scabbard and sawed through the zip-tie burning his wrists.

It popped open and he grabbed the dead man's Makarov pistol in a second, rolling over and using the corpse as a shield.

A figure darted out, trying to run, hands behind his back, screaming. Anda.

"Get down!"

He wouldn't listen. Or couldn't.

Blackwood saw Beria notice the fleeing man with a snort of disgust, as if he were a deserting private. He shot him in the back.

Anda fell dead.

Jaske screamed.

Blackwood fired off two shots at Beria, but he'd already ducked out of sight.

Exposed in the pool of light, he rolled into the darkness and surveyed the flashes of gunfire. Shots were coming in from two points: a pair of snipers who'd set up a pincer attack. The Russians fired back, but it was hopeless.

"Jaske!" he yelled.

She raised her head, trying to locate the voice above the crackle of deafening gunfire.

"Come here! Quick!"

She got to her knees and scooted blindly across the snow, skirting the pool of light.

Blackwood held her head down, jumped over her to shield her, and commenced fire.

He took out one of the tires of jeep — the police SUV — with a pleasing pop and fired off a steady succession of shots. Just enough to keep them from returning fire.

The Russians were caught in triangulation now.

Shouts of panic. Car doors clunked. They were opting for escape. Half the lights went off. No, they were turning off the headlights that marked their position and made them easier targets. Clever.

He shot into the side of the jeep and heard a scream.

The engine roared and the jeep pulled away.

"Curtis!"

Beria screamed after them and shot into the night. A man betrayed.

But a man silhouetted against the light.

Blackwood double-tapped and Beria fell.

A volley of shots thundered from the snipers, punctuated by screams and the thud of men falling in the snow.

And it all fell silent, but for the sound of Curtis's jeep roaring out there somewhere in the dark.

He thought of the snowmobile and giving chase, but to stand right now might mean a bullet through the head.

Did the snipers know them? Was this a rescue mission? Could they recognize them, even with the thermal night vision sights they must be using. He wasn't going to test it.

"Are you all right?" He patted Jaske on the back.

"Yes. I think."

Another shot echoed in the distance.

Blackwood glanced up.

Out there. A shot at the fleeing jeep. Whoever it was, they were making sure no one left the scene.

The snowmobile was behind the lavvus. It was now or never. If they stayed here, whoever was out there would come and shoot anyone left alive.

"*Áhttje!*" Jaske shouted.

"Shhhh! What are you doing?"

She got to her knees and shouted again. *"Áhttje!"*

A voice came from out there, a sonorous man's cry. "Jaske!"

Her father.

Jaske shouted a stream of Sámi.

His footsteps came running, steady but cautious. He would be holding his rifle poised to fire and wary of tripping.

Blackwood trained his pistol on the remaining vehicles, ready to shoot anything that moved.

But there was no sound at all.

Then the sound, no, the sensation, the feeling, that someone was close. Someone breathing.

A man standing right over him. A man who had emerged from the dark without a sound.

A man who was pointing a hunting rifle right at Blackwood's head.

It wasn't Jaske's father.

54

THE MAN WAS AS old as Jaske's father, but with no white beard, only straggly, muddy hair that stuck out from under his blue cap. Traditional Sámi dress but faded and worn.

Jaske barked out instructions in Sámi.

The man lowered his rifle, and as he did so, another man with a rifle emerged from the darkness.

Guhtur.

"Áhttje!" Jaske shouted, running to his embrace.

The other man did not take his eyes off Blackwood, rifle lowered but still poised.

Blackwood held his arms out by his sides, palms open.

"Viggu!" Guhtur said. *"Dette er herre Blackwood."*

Viggu lowered his rifle and nodded.

Blackwood got to his feet.

"Mr Blackwood," Guhtur said. "This is my friend, Viggu. I went to get him, to ask his help." He turned to Jaske. "Where is your mother?"

"At home. Anda said she was safe."

Guhtur turned to his son's body lying face down in the snow, a dark stain spreading out under him.

"At least he did one good thing."

He kneeled and tousled Anda's mop of dark hair and let out a low moan of despair.

No. It was a song. He sang a *joik* for his dead son. Jaske and Viggu bowed their heads.

Blackwood glanced to where he thought the horizon might be, suppressing the urge to give chase. Curtis was out there, getting further and further away with every second.

The old man stopped singing and just stared at his son for a while. Then he said, "My son is dead."

He picked him up, grunting with the effort, held him in his arms and carried him to his lavvu.

They watched silently as he put him down at the opening and dragged him inside. He shuffled around and then the walls of the tent glowed a little, the fire crackling and hissing.

Jaske snatched up her Makarov from the snow and marched over to Beria's body.

The dead Russian stared up at her, as if caught sleeping and about to shout a complaint at being disturbed. She muttered something Blackwood couldn't hear and then shot a ragged red hole in his face. His body jerked in protest and his head lolled to one side, ruined, obscene.

Blackwood crept towards her, intending to take the gun from her. She was wasting ammunition they might need.

But one shot was enough. She wiped her nose and jammed the gun into her belt.

"I was going to spit on him but didn't want to leave my DNA."

Guhtur emerged, wiping tears from his face, and to Jaske's questioning gaze he simply said, "I want him to be warm when he goes to *Rotaimo.*"

"What do we do?" Jaske asked, hugging herself.

"It is over," Guhtur said. "Let us bury them and end this."

"We don't have time for that," Blackwood said. "Curtis could be across the border by now. He could be already in Linhammar."

Guhtur looked to his friend. "What do I care of that? Look at all the death that is here now. You have brought it to this place. My family's sacred place."

"*Ahttja*, no," Jaske said.

"He brought them here. Our *storjunkare* is stained with blood now."

"Don't blame him. It wasn't his fault."

Guhtur rounded on her, tears in his eyes, spittle frothing at his lips. "You called him Death! You brought him here!"

"No," she said, pointing at her father's lavvu. "Anda brought Death here. My brother. Your son. He sold his sister like a sack of foot-fur and he brought these monsters to his family's *storjunkare*. *He* brought death here, not Blackwood."

The old man slumped, as if all the rage took flight from his body and there was nothing left inside.

"I'm sorry," Blackwood said. "I'm truly sorry for your loss. But we don't have time for this. I know what Curtis is going to do."

"Blackwood, we don't care," said Jaske, and she looked at her feet; couldn't look him in the eye. "He's gone. Gone for good now. My father is right. It's over."

Blackwood shook his head. "No, what he's going to do... I think... This affects us all."

Guhtur clapped a giant hand on Blackwood's shoulder. "You saved my daughter, and for this I will always be in your debt. But your war with this evil man is yours. Only yours." He glanced back at his daughter. "She is my only child now. I will keep her safe."

"You can't," Blackwood said. "None of you are safe."

There was no time for this. He marched over to the vehicles. The border police SUV had its tyres shredded. Some idiot had shot them to ribbons.

He turned his attention to the Russian Hunter LAV. It was a bit shot up, but the tyres seemed intact. Scattered all around were the bodies of dead Russians. The tyre tracks of Curtis's jeep curved away into the dark like an invitation.

"Blackwood!" Jaske called. "What is it?"

Machine guns scattered all around. He scooped them up and threw them into the rear canopy of the jeep.

"Ask him," he said, jerking his thumb at Viggu. "Ask him about Linhammar."

"What happened?" Jaske asked.

The old man spat. "One of our planes — a Norwegian plane — lost its way. The Russians shot it down. We had to go in and rescue them. Out on the German Peninsula."

As Viggu went on with his story, Blackwood picked the bodies for other loot: spare magazines for the Kalashnikovs, a few more Makarovs, every spare bit of ammo he could find.

"I was a scout, because I knew the area well," said Viggu. "They put me with a British unit. SAS."

"A British unit," Jaske said. "Out here?"

"It was a NATO exercise. War games. Because the British were in the area, they asked them to go in and rescue the Norwegian crew. So we went in and got them. And then we were bombed, attacked by fighter jets. They killed almost everyone. The Norwegian crew, most of the British unit."

"Fucking Russians," Guhtur said.

"No. It was the Americans."

Blackwood paused in unbuckling a dead Russian's utility belt.

"The Americans bombed and shot the shit out of us," Viggu continued. "It was a mix up. They call it 'friendly fire' now, I think. It was a slaughterhouse. Our own allies, killing *us*. They covered it all up. It never happened."

So that was what had eaten Curtis up all these years. Another classic tale of betrayal and cover up.

"And it happened at Linhammer," Blackwood said. It wasn't a question.

They looked to him.

"You knew this?" Jaske asked.

Blackwood shook his head. "Curtis said 'the world will know the name *Linhammar.*' He said I wouldn't get to see the Northern Lights. He said they were going to be the brightest ever tonight."

"Maybe not tonight," Guhtur said. "There is too much cloud."

"He's going to make his own light show."

"A bomb?" Jaske asked.

"A bomb big enough to light the entire sky. Think about it. What kind of bomb could do that?"

"A nuke? Are you saying he has a nuke?"

"It's the only thing I can think of," Blackwood said. "He's going to do it on Russian soil. He'll probably try to implicate Norway. He's going to start a world war. And all to get revenge for what happened at Linhammar."

"Jesus," Jaske said.

"And if we don't stop him," Blackwood said. "This place is going to be another Chernobyl. You can say goodbye to your Sápmi. No other country will be claiming your land because it will be a dead zone."

Blackwood stood and strapped the dead Russian's utility belt around his waist. "So, do you want to stop him, or are you just gonna stay here and pray?"

55

J ASKE LOOKED TO HER father, but he was already stepping forward, his chest puffed out.

"I am Sámi," he said. "I will defend this land to my dying breath. And if that is tonight, then it will be tonight."

He clasped his rifle across his chest to emphasize the point.

Viggu stepped by his side. "Me too."

Jaske scooped up her Makarov pistol. "Don't you even think about telling me to stay here. I'm coming too."

"Jaske, no—" Guhtur said.

"*Ahttja*," Jaske said. "I'm not a girl who will stay in the kitchen making blood cakes while the men go off to fight. You know that. I am the daughter you raised."

"Yes, I know, but—"

"And I have been fighting this man since I was taken, and when it comes to the end, I want to be there to put a bullet through his head for what he's done to me. To *me.*"

Tears sprang to her eyes and she choked them back, rage burning in her soul. Hatred for what those men had put her through. She knew now she wanted to be the one to kill him.

Blackwood cast his eyes over the dead bodies scattered all around, like he was looking for something; something he might have forgotten. Another piece of the jigsaw to put together.

"What is it?" Jaske asked.

He went to Eriksen's corpse and rooted in his pockets, pulling out a mobile phone. He tossed it to Jaske. "Can you make this work?"

"You don't know how to operate a phone?"

"I'm out of practice."

She thumbed its screen to reveal a padlock symbol and the words *Use fingerprint to unlock.*

Eriksen's dead eyes stared up at the sky.

With a shiver of disgust, she bent down to the dead cop, picked up his cold hand, cupping it and placing his index finger on the sensor on the back of the phone. The screen lit up. "There we go."

She dropped his dead hand, stood, and cupped the phone.

Blackwood gazed on her with a wry smile. Was it admiration?

"First thing is to get that fingerprint lock off," she said, "so it doesn't shut down again."

"We could chop his hand off and take it with us," Blackwood said.

She wrinkled her nose. He was joking, but the thought of it...

She thumbed through to Settings, the Lock Screen menu and took off the fingerprint security. "Here we go. No more locks."

"Great. Now see if there's a number for Curtis. They must have been in touch all this time."

She scrolled through more screens. "Wait a minute. This looks like..."

"What is it?"

"I'm just looking through all the apps he has open and this one's a GPS map." A green and indigo map with a blue dot and a red dot pulsing, moving. She showed him the screen. "It looks like a tracker."

"What?" Blackwood took the phone and observed the red dot pulsing steadily away from the static blue dot. "Is that Curtis?"

"Maybe Eriksen put a tracker on Curtis's phone, so he'd always know where he was. A cop could do that if he gets clearance to monitor someone he says is engaged in suspicious cross-border activity."

"Stingray tech," Viggu said. "They use it to spy on Norwegian politicians. It was all over the news. He just says this number might be a smuggler and he gets a tracker on him."

"Maybe Eriksen wasn't so stupid after all," Jaske said.

There were no more bodies to strip of ammo. Blackwood opened the back of the Hunter jeep and threw the stash of arms in the back. He paused and whistled and picked up a particular weapon.

"Fuck," he said.

"Is that a machine gun?" Jaske asked.

"It's a shotgun. Kind of. Saiga-12."

He handled it like he wanted to sleep with it. Jaske thought of their lovemaking, interrupted by those bastards coming across the tundra, and felt a flutter of desire in her womb. She brushed the feeling aside with a barb, as she always did. "Is it making you hard? It looks like it's making you hard."

Blackwood just smirked. "Let's just say it evens things up a little."

Guhtur and Viggu climbed in the front.

"We need to go," Guhtur called. "He's well ahead of us."

Jaske climbed in the back and sat with Eriksen's phone on her lap. Blackwood bounced in and slumped facing her, a stash of weapons at their feet between them.

Guhtur revved the engine and powered the jeep off across the plain, following the tracks left by the maniac Jaske needed to kill.

56

BLACKWOOD TRIED TO SEE where they were going but it was difficult. A flash of a forest, a vast dark patch of a fjord only visible because of the moonlight on the surface, a bank of snow that almost tipped the jeep over, so that Jaske fell into his lap. They stared at each other for a few moments before the Hunter righted itself and she fell back. Somehow, Guhtur knew where they were going and sensed the terrain instinctively.

As they drove on along a winding path, Jaske tapped at the phone on her knee; not the mapping screen that showed where Curtis was but something else, scrolling through pages of text and pictures.

"What is that?" he asked.

"There's a lot of Twitter traffic about the Norwegian military implicated in smuggling and human trafficking and trying to blame it on the poor, innocent Russians. Norwegian terrorist cells, that kind of thing."

She showed him the screen but he couldn't make much of it; a confusing swirl of text and the kind of symbols you never used on a keyboard.

"Look at the hashtags. *#NORterrorists*. Hundreds of them."

"What's a hashtag?"

"You don't know anything about social media, do you?"

"I've been away a long time."

"Hashtags are little subjects that people talk about. If you want to talk about the same thing, there's a hashtag for it. The Russians have these troll farms. Thousands of people whose job is to flood the West with misinformation. Negative shit like this. Stir up hate and mistrust."

"Psyops," Blackwood said, pleased that he could connect. "Black propaganda."

"They do it on social media now," Viggu called back from the front seat. "They do it all over the Twitter and Facebook. They pollute our social media, hack our political system. It's all deflection, to obscure the truth with conspiracy theories and cynicism."

This was the new dirty war. It used to be that you broadcast radio to the enemy, or dropped leaflets behind enemy lines, and that was just the official stuff, not the off-the-books stuff that Clocktower had been involved in — the really dirty stuff. How much more refined it was now. The enemy was on your phone, whispering in your ear all the time. The enemy was playing you like a fucking banjo.

"But he'll need more than a Twitter rumour," said Jaske, "if he is going to implicate Norway in this sabotage. He will need some real physical proof."

"He'll find a way," Blackwood said. "He's a cunning bastard. Maybe he's set up some trail to a Norwegian. He has enough of them."

"How many Norwegians were involved in the kidnapping?" Guhtur asked.

"There was Nikolas and Orvik," Jaske said.

"Both criminals," said Blackwood, dismissing them.

"There was Pretke," Jaske suggested. "Wasn't he military?"

Blackwood nodded.

"And another called Rongstad," Jaske said.

"You knew him?"

"He was part of the crew. But he never came back from that first stop."

"He got slotted in Macduff," Blackwood said, "where they were going to bring you and the girls ashore and sell you off."

"Slotted?"

"Killed."

"By who?"

"By me."

"So when you say he got slotted, you mean you killed him?"

"Yes. That's pretty much it. I knew him from way back. In Sierra Leone, and Ramala."

"You've never explained how you came to be in the hands of this criminal gang with a bullet in you."

"It's a long story. If we get out of this, I'll tell you all about it."

They fell silent and Blackwood gave his attention to the distant ache of doubt that had been nagging at the edge of his consciousness for hours; only just seeing it. What if it wasn't Pretke or Rongstad that Curtis was using. What if it was everyone in this jeep. Three Norwegian nationals and an Englishman. What if this was all part of Curtis's plan —

to lure them in only to frame them for the terrorist atrocity he was about to commit.

Was that why Twitter was buzzing with gossip about Norwegian terrorists hitting Russia. Could Curtis have prepared it this much, even with Russian cooperation? Did the Russians know his plan and were willing to stage this atrocity to provoke a war and split Europe and NATO. Would it all come out afterwards — the details of this terror gang — two disaffected Sámi rebels, father and daughter, and a dead son and brother who'd been involved in smuggling drugs and human trafficking. An ex-army scout who'd survived a friendly fire fuck up, old and bitter and out for revenge.

And a disaffected Brit, ex-Pathfinder, dishonourably discharged, ex-con and recently responsible for a terrorist attack in Scotland.

Could Curtis have planned it all out to such a degree? Was he that clever?

Were they only pawns in his game? Were they doing exactly as he wanted and framing themselves as the terrorists?

He shook his head, trying to get Curtis out. He was thinking like that madman, maybe even thinking way too much like him, beyond what even Curtis was capable of thinking. This was how a lunatic got inside you — he had you thinking insane thoughts, thinking diabolical things even he couldn't imagine. The psychopath dragged you into his cesspit.

"When do we reach the border?" Blackwood asked.

"We crossed it ten minutes ago," Guhtur said.

Blackwood laughed. The border really didn't exist for the Sámi. "Are we going to encounter any military?"

"There is nothing much here," Viggu said. "Linhammar is a military base. Kind of. Enough to be important, but not enough to be so well guarded. There's a diving centre down the coast and that is bigger."

It really was the arse end of Russia, the borders patrolled by a gang of disaffected rabble who were more interested in smuggling than enemy invasion.

"He's stopped," Jaske said.

57

BLACKWOOD SCOOTED OVER TO sit beside her. She pinched the screen to zoom out and show the throbbing red dot of Curtis and the moving blue dot that was this jeep, this phone, closing in.

"Where is it?"

"There's an old abandoned German post about a kilometre north of the diving centre."

The satellite image showed a cluster of buildings on the estuary coast, almost a village, and as the coast opened out to a giant bay there was evidence of a harbour and a Naval History Museum marked. Inland from that was a cluster of buildings in the wild, almost like a plan of an old Roman settlement. The satellite image was all green, showing forest and sunlight casting long shadows of trees, but of course, it wouldn't be like that; now it was all snow and ice and no sun to cast any shadows, only a pale moon to light the way.

"That's not right," Viggu said.

"Why not?"

"The plane came down about a half kilometre north-east of here. It's that direction."

"But the snows have changed everything," said Blackwood. "How can you tell, after all these years?"

Viggu turned in his seat and fixed Blackwood with an even gaze. "I am Sámi, and this is the Sápmi. I know this land like my wife's body and she has been dead for many years."

"But the signal says he's there," Jaske said, pointing the way her father had already veered the jeep towards.

"It doesn't make sense," Viggu answered. "Surely he would want to go to the exact spot."

"Maybe he doesn't know the land as well as you," Blackwood said. "Maybe he just knows it's somewhere near here."

Viggu shrugged.

"We have to go with the signal."

Guhtur put his foot down and the Hunter roared on through the darkness.

Through the side windows, Blackwood could see they were moving along a road, long since snowed over, that ran through vast acres of forest, the trees bare. Moonlight bounced off the ice and snow and illuminated everything icy blue, like the land was already irradiated. A haunted, spectral landscape.

He wondered for a wild moment if Curtis had already detonated his bomb. But they would have heard it, felt it, surely.

The Hunter passed a single concrete block of a building on the road and Blackwood trained his Saiga-12 on it, ready to return any sniper fire. But they passed by safely and turned a bend. While they were on this road, they were sitting ducks.

"It's here," Guhtur said, turning right and slowing to a crawl.

"The signal is in a building 470 metres south of here," Jaske said.

"We get out here," said Blackwood.

Guhtur killed the engine and they were overwhelmed by a deathly silence.

They piled out of the jeep and Blackwood dumped the bag of weapons on the ice.

Crowding around Jaske, they surveyed the map on her phone, trying to place it to the terrain. Over to the south-east a low hill like a bluff. To the west, a path curled around, screened by trees, which would afford another covering position.

"Guhtur, you take the hill. Viggu, this path to the west. Pincer movement."

He thought to explain what that was, but they knew. They'd performed exactly the same manoeuvre an hour ago.

"If you get any shot. Take it. Don't hesitate."

"Don't worry," said Guhtur, "we won't."

Blackwood nodded and smiled by way of apology. They'd shown at the *storjunkare* just how ruthless they could be.

The two old men set off and, in a moment, Blackwood and Jaske were alone.

"What do we do?" Jaske asked.

"We go to the front door and knock."

"Okay," she said simply.

"You've got a Makarov?"

Jaske took it out from her belt.

"When we get close enough, lose the phone. You'll need two hands."

He delved into the bag of weapons and pulled out a couple of spare mags for the Makarov and tossed them to her. "Keep these in the same pocket, so you know where to go to reload. Muscle memory."

He pulled out a Kalashnikov and put it over her head to strap it to her back. "And here. Two spare mags for that." He shoved them into the opposite pocket. "If we come under fire, just give it all you've got."

She nodded.

He wondered for a moment about telling her to stay here and guard the jeep, but it was useless. She wouldn't do it, and even if she did, she was safer with him.

"Okay," he said, "let's do it."

They set off along the icy path that wound its way southwards, thankful for the screen of trees. If this had been a proper exercise, he would have scouted the surroundings first. The map is not the land, he'd always learned. You needed to do due reconnaissance. But there was no time. Curtis could detonate his nuke at any moment.

They passed the rusted battlements and the derelict metal and concrete of former gun positions, faded and forlorn like the bones of dinosaurs strewn along a desolate coast. An empire in ruins.

He consulted the screen Jaske held out, tracking their progress with the blue dot, until they were almost on top of the red dot of Curtis inside that building.

Somewhere out there in the dark, on that hill to the east and through those trees to the west, Guhtur and Viggu had them in their sights.

"Phone off," Blackwood said.

Jaske pressed a button and the light died.

58

BLACKWOOD TRIED TO THINK back to the moment Curtis had fled. In the confusion of a hail of bullets, he'd jumped in a Hunter with how many goons? Was it two? Or just one?

He replayed the scene but could see it both ways. His imagination had usurped his memory. It was no good. There were two, possibly three guns trained on their approach right now and they would soon start firing.

The building was a hundred yards down a path, lit by moonlight reflecting on snow, and Blackwood could see now that it was little more than an abandoned concrete bunker, the windows just crumbling holes, rafters exposed like the rib cage of a battlefield corpse.

There was no way they could approach without being seen. All they had was the cover from Guhtur and Viggu.

No way to contact them and tell them to unleash a volley of covering fire.

"Here goes," Blackwood said.

"What?" Jaske asked.

He broke into a quick march, holding the Saiga-12 firmly locked in his shoulder, keeping it trained on the building. He pulled the trigger and felt it almost knock him off his feet. One of the dark windows became a ragged great hole, masonry falling.

He marched on, shooting every second, taking giant lumps out of the building, a volley of fire that matched his tread.

Covering fire came in from both sides. Guhtur and Viggu.

The building was peppered with shots, clouds of dust exploding all around the black windows. No one could respond.

Breath taut, Blackwood scampered the last few steps to the building and right through the black mouth of the door, only wondering at the final second if there really was a door. He flying-kicked at it and sailed right inside, skidding on slates and shooting a few rounds into the rafters.

The shooting ceased. Viggu and Guhtur would not risk covering fire now he was inside. They would come running.

Footsteps came crunching on ice behind him and the rasp of ragged breath. Jaske.

Blackwood jumped to his knees and scoped the building, ready to take out anyone who might have her in their sights.

But there was no one.

"Blackwood!"

She came running in and skidded on the slates.

Blackwood held out an arm and caught her.

Still for a moment. The place was empty.

"But he's here," Jaske said. "The phone says he's here."

Someone cackled.

Blackwood spun, his shotgun trained on the intruder.

A phone sitting on a rickety old wooden chair.

He stepped towards it, rifle still trained, ready to shoot anyone who moved.

But it was just a phone. The display revealed a Union Jack screensaver.

"Shit," said Jaske. "He knows we're tracking him."

"That's right," the tinny voice crackled again. "Hey, Blackwood. Having trouble finding me?"

A dozen scenarios flashed through Blackwood's mind, and all of them screamed *Get out.*

The phone could detonate a bomb, the place could be booby trapped, having drawn them to this spot, Curtis and his men might now fire on them.

He grabbed Jaske's arm and propelled her back out of that door.

The crackle of Curtis's laughter chased them out and the last thing he heard were the words, "Don't worry. I wouldn't kill you here and spoil all the fun!"

As they bolted up the path, Blackwood checked the skyline and shouted, "Run!' as loud as he could.

If Guhtur and Viggu were approaching, they would retreat.

He ran with Jaske, expecting a blast of heat on his back at any second, but in no time at all they were cowering by the Hunter.

Guhtur and Viggu came running in from east and west, both panting at the effort.

"He wasn't there," Jaske called. "Just the phone. It was a trap."

But no, it wasn't, Blackwood thought. Curtis could have set a trap and killed them so easily. This was something else. This was a game.

Curtis couldn't do it now. Unless he'd led them to his suitcase nuke and was already speeding away from its flashpoint. But surely, Curtis knew this was a mission he wouldn't survive?

The phone in Jaske's hand bleated and woke. She let out a little scream.

A Union Jack logo on the screen.

Jaske stroked the screen a couple of times and Curtis's voice fizzled to life so they could all hear it.

"I could have had you quite easily there, Blackwood. You ought to know better than to walk into a trap like that."

Jaske held the phone in the air so Blackwood could speak.

"What I'm thinking," Blackwood said, "is how are you getting out of this, Curtis? When you detonate that suitcase nuke of yours, you're going to have to be at least a hundred kilometres away when it blows. If you want to survive."

A blast of static. A choke of surprise. Then Curtis said, "Maybe I don't want to survive."

"Of course you do, Curtis. What's the point of going to all this trouble if you're not around to see it?"

There was no answer, just the hiss of static. But Blackwood thought he could hear the madman's manic grin.

"What use is revenge like this if you're not there to see it? You're not going to kill yourself in the act. You have to see how you've fooled everyone. That's the whole point. That's what every psychopath lives for."

Again the silence, but this time tense. Blackwood might be imaging it but he thought the smile was gone now and there was just rage on the other end.

When Curtis's voice came, it was quite calm, as if this were a point of principle and he was only concerned that the truth be put on record. "All special ops personnel are high-functioning psychopaths, Blackwood. You know that. We're the same."

"If I was the same as you, I wouldn't be out here promising to put a bullet through your fucking brain."

"How charming. You don't really have the intellect to see things with clarity, Blackwood. You've always been too blunt an instrument. You thought the drugs operation through Norway was all your idea. But it was mine. I put you in a place where you'd make that connection. Just like I put you in a criminal gang, like I put you in a two-bit doorman's job. Like I put some feral youth in your face so you'd almost kill him and get your dishonourable discharge. You think you've been making decisions, Blackwood, but I've been pulling your strings for a decade or more."

A sickening, woozy sensation in the pit of his stomach, like a plane dropping from the sky.

"That's right," Curtis said. "I knew you'd go to Rongstad with your idea. I've been programming you all this time, and I even brought you right here. You're here because of me. Think about that."

"You're full of shit, Curtis."

His own voice sounded weak, wounded, even to himself. His finger tightened on the trigger of the Saiga-12. He took it off and pointed it firmly at the ground.

"Don't be too upset, Blackwood. You're just a puppet in a game that started long before you were ever aware of it."

"Yeah, yeah, 1970, we all know about that. Move on, for fuck's sake."

Again, Curtis laughed. "You think it's about that. No, that was just the seed. It all really began after 9/11."

What was this? More psychopathic nonsense.

"When the world was gathering for the first minute's silence, someone went to a cyber cafe in Oxford and posted a poem to an alt/conspiracy site. I saw the potential even then. The power of the lie. That you could move people with a strong enough lie."

"That's nothing new, Curtis, you thick bastard. You didn't invent propaganda."

"No, but I invented fake news. Take a look at the fucking world; the West is falling apart, putting a gun to its own head because it thinks its head is its enemy. The Russians tried to bring the West down for years. The West thought they'd won and the Russians were finished. I taught them how to win the Cold War with a fucking tweet. Tell me I didn't change the world. I knew the Cold War could be won with data, not bullets and bombs. I did that."

"And here you are, out in the wilderness — a madman with bullets and bombs."

Curtis's voice came back too quickly; petulant, stung. "That was just the starter. Wait till you see what's next on the menu."

Blackwood smiled. He'd needled him. "So you're going to start World War Three, all because you botched some mission years ago? Is it worth it?"

"They lied to us, Blackwood. You know that more than anyone. They tore you apart with lies. The army dumped your sorry fucking arse at the first whiff of scandal. That's what they do."

"They didn't do that to me. *You* did that."

"I showed you the truth behind the lie."

And the line went dead. The anonymous outline in Jaske's palm went blank and left the words *Call Ended*. The sociopath, laughing at how he'd fooled everyone.

And he became aware of something outside himself, something outside the sickening swoon of dread that drowned him.

It was Jaske's face.

She stared at him. The cold look of someone betrayed.

"Jaske. You have to know. I was the one who suggested the route. Of a drugs operation. And yes, I'm ashamed of that. But you heard what he did to me. He destroyed everything so the only option I had in life was to join a criminal gang. I would never have suggested trafficking people, women. I'm not a fucking psychopath."

"Aren't you, Blackwood? I don't see much difference."

"Jaske," Guhtur said. "We have to work together. You can argue later."

Jaske looked away, her eyes burning a hole in the snow at her feet.

"Believe me, Jaske," Blackwood said. "I didn't know about the girls. The drugs deal was my idea a long time ago. Ten years ago, before they framed me and put me in prison. I went to Macduff to smash it up. I went there to kill them all. And that's how I ended up here."

Jaske shook her head and finally looked at him, and now that gaze was burning a hole through him. "What kind of man are you?" she said. "I should have left you to die."

"Come," said Viggu, a keen edge of desperation in his voice. "We must go. Now."

"Where?" Blackwood asked.

"I told you," Viggu said. "A half mile north of here."

The old man pointed over the brow of a dark, snow-covered hill.

They piled into the Hunter and Blackwood threw the bag of weapons between him and Jaske.

She folded her arms tightly across her belly and wouldn't look at him, as the jeep roared to that dark hill.

59

BLACKWOOD CRANED HIS NECK to try to see the landscape as the jeep bumped and rocked along rough terrain. It was all snow but he could sense they were off-road now, if there were anything in this wilderness you could even call a road.

They seemed about to reach the foot of the hill and launch themselves up its steep incline when Viggu barked some instruction and Guhtur pulled up and left the engine humming, the headlights illuminating a bank of snow.

Viggu jumped out and peered at the ground before them.

"What is it?" Blackwood asked.

"He reads the snow," Guhtur said.

Viggu looked both ways, nodded to himself and jumped back in.

"What?" Blackwood asked.

"They went that way," he said, pointing right. "So we go the other way round."

"Are you sure?"

"Their tracks take that route. The wreck is just around there. No one got out, so we're safe to go this way. Trust me." Viggu threw in a confident smile.

Blackwood shook his head and smiled too, grateful for a morsel of levity to cut the ice between him and Jaske.

"I never trust anyone who says, 'trust me'."

He couldn't help it. He glanced at Jaske and caught her permafrost glare.

He'd said it to her. He'd said *trust me,* and now he'd betrayed her.

Guhtur turned left and the Hunter wound its way through a ravine, rocky walls on both sides of the jeep, so close you could reach out and scrape your fingers. The kind of place you could easily be attacked. Perilous. Exposed. No way out. The jeep rocked side to side.

Jaske wrapped her arm tightly in a cord that hung from the roof, gritting her teeth, determined not to fall against him. She was done with that. That one spark of human connection. He was done with it too. It was for the best. She was right: he was a monster; he belonged with the likes of Curtis, with the monsters, in the shadows. He didn't belong with decent human beings. He'd go to his death now and take one of those monsters with him. It was all he was good for. And if he came out of it, the best thing to do was walk away forever and shun all human contact.

They came out of the ravine to open terrain and he breathed again. A path that curved, still bumpy beneath them so not a road, maybe a reindeer track.

He set his eyes on the road ahead. It was a long, dead road, and it led only to destruction. But he gritted his teeth so hard his jaw ached. He was going to walk into the flames.

They came to a low crest, a snow bluff that might have been a snowdrift anywhere else but was clearly a ridge.

"It's here," Viggu said, with a sad note of reflection; a man returning to bad memories.

Guhtur killed the jeep and they jumped out.

Viggu went straight to the ridge, flopped face down and peered over with night vision binoculars.

Blackwood dumped the bag of weapons at Viggu's feet and flopped down beside him, the Saiga-12 at his side.

"The wreck is two hundred meters straight ahead," Viggu said.

He handed Blackwood the binoculars. They turned the midnight blue landscape into a glowing green seabed. A strange shape in the snow, like a white draped dead bird, like a broken umbrella.

"The plane. It's still here?" Blackwood said.

Viggu shrugged. "They would have stripped it long ago, but I guess no one was bothered to move it."

Curtis was inside it, that much was certain.

Did he even have anyone with him? Or was it now just Curtis vs Blackwood — the master versus the disciple?

Jaske took the binoculars to look for herself.

Blackwood took one last look at her, drank her in, the woman who'd saved his life; the woman Blackwood had put in the hands of these monsters. He'd denied it: he was nowhere near the scene of the crime and his fingerprints weren't on the weapon. But he knew, and she knew he was guilty. He'd commissioned the crime. She was right. He was a monster just like the rest of them; the whole dirty, rotten criminal gang of monsters that preyed on the innocent.

There was only one thing to be done. With a flush of rage burning in his chest, Blackwood shot up and marched over the brow.

"Wait, what are you doing?" Guhtur said.

"Stay," Blackwood said. "This is between me and him."

60

HE RAISED THE SAIGA-12 to his shoulder and fired off an opening salvo which took a lump out of the old plane.

And the air exploded all around him, snow dancing around his boots. A bullet whistled past his cheek. An inch to one side and it would have ripped his ear off.

Two snipers, one at each end of the plane.

Shots came from behind him. Viggu and Guhtur. And Jaske too. Maybe she was laying covering fire and not shooting him in the back. Though he wouldn't blame her.

He marched on through the inferno, the Saiga-12 firmly packed against his shoulder, his shots matching the measured tread of his boots.

And for a moment he felt alive. Marching across open ground, like a tommy across No Man's Land with just a rifle in his hand. There was something exhilarating about it. Marching into the jaws of death screaming a great big fuck you to it all. This was life. In the midst of death. Like it said. Was it the Bible or Shakespeare? He wondered how he could have these wild thoughts while about to die.

Focus.

One of the snipers fell silent. He wasn't sure who'd got him.

He trained all his fire on the other one.

The Saiga took out a fucking great chunk of the plane and chunks of meat sprayed all over the snow. No more snipers. It was just Curtis now.

Curtis and a nuke. That was all.

He aimed at the centre of the plane, only presuming that was where Curtis was.

A fusillade of bullets came from the heart of the wreck. He was right. Curtis in the middle and a sniper at each end.

Blackwood fell to the snow.

Cold ice burned his face.

The wreck was peppered with a spray of return fire from the others behind him.

Blackwood didn't move for a few moments. It would be so easy to lie down here and die. But a spurt of pure hatred kindled in him. He sprang up, scooted for the wreck, and slammed against the frozen hull just to the side of the great opening where the plane had broken in half.

His Saiga trained on the rim of the hole, he edged forward, ready to shoot if Curtis popped out.

A hand came out and there was a flash of gunfire.

Blackwood, shot back, blind, and dropped to his knees. More shots from distance rattled the hull.

He crawled forward, praying for sight to return.

From the darkness emerged the blue snow and the dark wall of the wreck.

Curtis was on the other side. Blackwood put the shotgun to the hull and shot through it, punching holes clean through as he walked to the opening. If the covering fire kept Curtis inside, he'd be all right. If Curtis dared to jump out and shoot, Blackwood would be dead.

He shot and shot and shot until the Saiga-12 sputtered and gave a disappointing empty crack.

He threw it in the snow and pulled out two Makarovs and tried to count the bullets left. Enough, surely. And if not, there was the knife tucked into his boot.

Pumping both, he stormed through the hole, the muzzle flare illuminating the black interior like a firecracker.

Empty. Nothing but the damp decay of neglect and the shit of animals that had used it as a shelter.

Curtis was gone.

Blackwood pushed through to the other side.

The shooting from the others ceased and an eerie silence descended on everything.

An engine sputtered and roared. The UAZ Hunter.

Blackwood sprinted after it, shooting from both Makarovs, knowing he would have to ditch one or both if he wanted to grab hold and jump on.

The jeep achingly out of reach.

Something trailing on the ground. A length of blue nylon rope.

He ditched one of the Makarovs, dived and grabbed a hold, the rope burning through his grip for an agonizing second till he caught a knot and it pulled him.

Forlornly, he tried to shoot, as he was dragged. A bullet pinged off the rear chassis. More likely to ricochet through his brain.

With a scream of defiance, he pulled himself round and fought to raise himself, his knees screaming in protest.

And for a moment, he was jet skiing behind it, his boots sliding on ice, the rope taut, burning through his glove.

The ice slowed the jeep, or he'd be dead already. He pulled himself closer, pain exploding through his arms.

Just inches from the jeep.

He lurched forward and gripped the rear lip, abandoned the rope, his boots skidding on ice. One bump and the jeep would shake him off.

He heaved himself aboard and fell into the rear well, stunned like an abattoir cow with a bolt through its brain.

His wound unravelling. He'd been shot only, what? five days ago. The myriad fights since then flashed through his mind, each one a point of searing pain: the escape attempt on the island. Torture. Killing Orvik. The escape on the bus. The gunfight at the *storjunkare*. So many deaths flashing before his eyes.

Dizzy, losing it.

His face against a chrome suitcase propped open. A thick metal pipe lodged diagonally across the middle, a starter switch, a battery pack.

A fucking nuclear bomb.

He could toss it overboard. But what if it had a timer? Had Curtis primed it to go off? There was no handy countdown clock ticking down the seconds to Armageddon.

Curtis in the driver's seat. He could put a bullet through the back of his head right now, if only he could raise himself. He just wanted to die.

Pushing the pistol on the floor, he heaved himself up to his knees, swaying with the jeep and aimed the Makarov at Curtis.

The gun jerked left and right. He couldn't get a fix.

Curtis twisted back in his seat and shot behind him. The interior of the jeep resonated with a colossal boom.

Blackwood's ears rung.

A bullet hole through the roof of the cabin.

The jeep rocked and jolted so much, Curtis had to grip the steering wheel with both hands, one holding his pistol.

Another shot boomed and the windscreen shattered. Curtis dropped the pistol that had gone off in his hand with a jolt over the terrain.

Blackwood pounced up and aimed. Here it was, shoot him in the back. Finish him for good.

The jeep bounced and Blackwood smashed against the wall, struggled to right himself and aimed again.

With a scream, Curtis left the steering wheel, and turned, lunging over the seat.

Blackwood fell back, the old man screaming in his face.

He kicked him off and scrambled for his Makarov but it skittered away and out the rear of the jeep, careening off into the snow.

Curtis smacked into him, but Blackwood flipped him over. The old man flew into the front seat head first. For a moment he was just a tangle of legs in the air, then he righted himself and tried to scramble back. His pistol in his hand.

Blackwood stared, watching with a detached fascination.

The jeep cruised on.

Through the shattered windscreen, an expanse of clear ice, and something grey just beyond it.

The sea.

An ice-free harbour, they'd said.

Blackwood calculated the distance and realized they were gunning towards a cliff edge.

Curtis raised his gun and aimed.

The cliff edge hurtling towards them.

He should dive at the old man and disarm him.

Blackwood smiled.

Curtis, half over the seat, frowned and snarled.

Do the opposite.

Blackwood stepped back into a void and was weightless for a moment before he smacked into the hard ground. All the air left him.

He raised his head just as the Hunter UAZ sped over the cliff edge, floated in the air for a moment and plunged out of sight.

Blackwood held his breath, waiting for an explosion that would turn the night sky to daylight, an unforgettable fire that would incinerate him.

From beyond the cliff edge came a faint splosh.

Panting, breathing again, his head fell back and he stared at the lurid streaks of purple and green that danced with the stars. The Northern Lights.

61

A SEARING PAIN SCORCHED his shoulder, like someone was exploring his collarbone with a blowtorch.

He prised open his concrete eyelids and strained to see. A dark patch spreading across his chest. Bleeding. He'd been shot in the heart. No. The old wound had opened. Jaske's bad stitchwork had come undone. How fitting.

An engine drone thickened and grew louder, closer, in the howling wind. The jeep came crunching over ice and pulled up with a screech.

They had come to his aid.

"Blackwood?" Jaske said. There was a genuine note of concern in her voice, though he wouldn't blame her if she kicked his half-dead carcass over the cliff. He probably deserved it. He was worthless. A pariah. A devil. Everyone with good in their soul should shun him.

"He's alive," Guhtur said. "What were you thinking?"

His words caught in his throat, thick with blood. "I had to stop him. It was between me and him."

"It's not between you and him," Guhtur said. "Not when it's my homeland."

He tried to laugh but it hurt like hell. "Fair enough."

They sat him up and he leaned against someone's knees. Jaske's. Viggu looked out at the vast void. "Is he dead?"

"Nothing will survive that," Guhtur said.

"He might," said Blackwood. "You don't know him like I do."

"What about the bomb?" said Jaske. "It's sitting at the bottom of that bay."

"I imagine the Russians will know," said Viggu. "Somehow, they always do. They'll take care of it, quietly, and no one will ever know about it."

Jaske pressed her hands to Blackwood's shoulder and he let out an involuntary squeal.

"We patch him up in the car," Guhtur said. "We have to go."

Viggu and Guhtur took an arm each and hoisted him up. His head swam again and he thought he might pass out. They held him up and he took one last look out at that vast darkness. The cruel Barents wind howling in his face.

Curtis was out there. He couldn't be dead. Nothing would ever kill him.

They walked him to the car — two old men taking his weight, his boots floating an inch above the ice. They sat him on the lip of the jeep's rear.

Jaske jumped in and dragged him inside. He lay at her feet. The bag of weapons was on the seat now. He was lying where the weapons had lain. There was irony in that. That was all he was, at the end of it: just a useless bag of weaponry.

The car set off and he jostled against her boots, letting out another yelp at the pain.

Jaske knelt over him and took out a wad of something — her scarf, was it? — and jabbed it into his wound. Then she ripped off lengths of Gaffa tape with her teeth and stripped a cross over his heart. X marks the spot. But there was no treasure here. There was nothing here. This was a plague sign. Keep away. Death lives here.

At some point, he passed out. Sleep took him, slowly at first and then all at once, and he was so deep in slumber he didn't see when they crossed back over the border. Which was fitting. Because the border didn't exist for any of the people on this long road from Linhammar.

62

Tromsø was a huddle of small shopping streets edging a harbour, Christmas lights glowing on snow.

Blackwood tramped alongside Guhtur to the shopping centre that was just up the street a way, the frost clouding around his face, wincing at the discomfort around his bruised and sewn up torso.

"So, our friend is called Dag," Guhtur said. "He's transporting reindeer meat south. It's a 24-hour drive to Oslo, so you will stop for a sleep break at a rest stop halfway. But only for a couple of hours, he says."

"Sounds fine," Blackwood said.

He had heard the plan in detail for the last two days. Blackwood would accompany the freight driver on the trip to Oslo, all the way down the E6, including one ferry crossing. Once in Oslo, he could easily cross into Sweden and make his way to Malmö. He would cross the Øresund

Bridge to Denmark and from there it was a short route down to Germany. Easy to cross those Schengen borders. Less easy to get a fake passport and just fly from Oslo to London.

That was the story, anyway, and he was happy enough that Guhtur believed it.

From outside, the shopping centre looked no bigger than a cinema, but as they swept inside, to be greeted with a blast of warm air, the space opened out to a great atrium with balconies and escalators. A giant Christmas tree dominated the atrium and strings of fairy lights cascaded from the balconies. Still the festive decorations. It wasn't New Year's Eve yet.

Guhtur headed for a food hall, shopping list in hand.

"I need to get a phone," Blackwood said, scanning the place for a mobile store. "There's someone I need to call."

"You can use my phone," Guhtur said.

"It's okay. I need my own anyway."

Guhtur nodded, as if he understood and waved him away, disappearing in the food hall.

Blackwood headed for the mobile phone outlet. It was important he didn't use Guhtur's phone. Nothing that was traceable and might bring death on someone else. Curtis was dead. Beria was dead. They were all dead. But someone out there might still be chasing that ten million; might still be waiting for Blackwood to pop up on the system.

He asked the assistant for a burner phone, in English, knowing it wouldn't be a problem, and added, "With a prepaid sim, please. Ready to go, if you can."

The assistant gave him a neutral look, trying not to seem as if she was assessing how much of a criminal she was talking to. But she nodded, shrugged and took the phone out of its box, fiddling with the battery and setting it up.

Once it was done, he paid with a wad of Kroner and walked to the Christmas tree, finding a bench to sit on.

He called the only mobile number he'd ever remembered. The only one he'd ever had to remember.

The phone bleated in his ear and he held his breath, wondering if there would be an answer.

Someone picked up.

"Lola?" he said, and then cursed himself. He should have waited for her to speak. He was getting sloppy.

A stunned silence. Was that her breathing, or was it someone who had her phone? Had all of this been for nothing?

"Blackwood?" she said.

He breathed again. "Yes, it's me."

"Shit! I thought you were dead."

"So did I. Is all well?"

"Yes," she said. "Yes. We're safe."

He heaved a sigh of relief.

"There were a few hairy moments," she said, "but we're safe."

"Good."

"Where are you?"

"You wouldn't believe me. Norway."

"How the fuck?"

"It's a long story."

She was laughing. Or crying, he couldn't tell.

"Listen. I'm going to have to ask you to dip into some of that money. If you can."

"I think we can spare a little. What do you want?"

"A passport. A fake one. Not in my name. But you have a photo of me."

She thought about it for a while. He listened to her breathing. "I'll see what I can do."

"There's a man I think can do it." He gave her a name and an email address.

She wrote it down.

"And when you get it, I want you to post it to this post office box in Oslo."

He gave her the address and she added it to her notes.

"Thanks," he said.

They said goodbye.

"Wait. When will you be back?"

"I don't know," he said.

He hung up, shoved the phone in his jacket pocket and stood.

Guhtur came over with a single yellow plastic carrier bag and gave it to him. Provisions for the journey. "You got through to your friends? They can help?"

Blackwood nodded. There was no point telling him that he'd arranged for a passport to be sent to Oslo. Guhtur would only say he could have had it sent here. It was best he left them well alone and they never saw again. It was best that he did that with everyone in the world.

"Then let's go," Guhtur said.

They walked out to the freezing street and marched up the long road till it spilled out to a large open space where coaches and a red truck were parked.

Blackwood cast a glance at a newspaper display as they passed. He couldn't understand the words on the headlines, but most of the tabloids carried a photo from the TV footage of Jaske and the women huddled in the square at Kirkenes.

Guhtur stopped and smiled at the sight of his daughter all over the news. "It's a shame she couldn't be here to say goodbye," he said.

"It doesn't matter."

"She sang such a beautiful *joik* for you. A great honour."

"I know."

"Did you know a *joik* can be a courting ritual?"

"No, I didn't," Blackwood said, trying not to smile.

"But she also called you an angel of death. I don't think I like my daughter courting the angel of death."

"Neither do I," Blackwood said.

Guhtur waved to the truck. The driver flashed his headlights.

"Thank you for everything," Blackwood said.

"Thank you for bringing my daughter back to me," Guhtur said. "And everything else."

They shook hands and Blackwood turned away. He trotted across the open space to the truck and climbed into the cab.

The man called Dag smiled and nodded and turned the ignition. The truck hissed, roared and pulled away and in moments they had crossed the bridge to the mainland under cover of snow-topped mountains, and were on the long road south.

Thank You

... for reading *Cold Border*. If you liked it, please take a minute to write a review where you bought it. Reviews help us sell more books, and if that happens, John Blackwood will return in

DEATH IN OSLO

John Blackwood, seeking refuge, is thrust into Oslo's shadows as a series of brutal murders unravels the city's veneer of tranquility.

Turn the page for an exclusive extract.

1

AT FIRST IT WAS black and silent, as if they were not moving, as if they were trapped in a yawning cavern of Norwegian night. But then they were speeding on a cable-stayed bridge, the headlights of cars rushing in the opposite direction. A chasm of water under them, and for a moment it seemed they were under it, beneath the rushing ice-cold fjord. The air was cold and thin and all Blackwood could think as he was rushing through it was what this monstrous bridge must have cost: the oil and concrete, the steel and the human reputation, the vast sums of money poured into its construction.

And then he was there, in the middle of the bridge, looking down at the water below. It was then that he saw his daughter, standing on the edge of the bridge, ready to jump. Blackwood's heart dropped. He ran towards her, but the bridge seemed to stretch forever, and he couldn't reach her in time.

She jumped, and Blackwood woke up with a jolt.

The truck had come to a stop again. He blinked and nodded to Dag, who did not return his smile. For two days, on the long, slow drive from Tromso, all the way down the strip of land that was Norway, Dag had smiled but said little.

Blackwood peered out at the dim sodium light of an industrial estate.

"Is this Oslo?"

Dag shook his head. "Almost. This is Stovner. One stop before Oslo."

Dag jumped out of the cab and walked off to a line of industrial units.

Blackwood pulled up his phone and hit the Maps icon. A blue dot zoomed in on their location. They were 13 kilometres from Oslo central, only 20 minutes away. It didn't make sense that they would stop for another rest this close to their destination.

He sighed and stretched. Maybe this was Dag's delivery drop off and the end of the road. Maybe this was where Blackwood would have to get off and make his own way into Oslo. Or maybe Dag would be charitable and drive the twenty minutes and drop him off in the centre. He was at the man's mercy.

Blackwood peered out through the murky orange glow over this industrial estate. There was no sound apart from the distant hum of traffic and the pitter-patter of raindrops on the truck.

He could make out Dag approaching a group of dark figures in the distance. Something about them, the dark clothes, the casual sports gear they all wore, something about the way they lurked, made the hair tingle on Blackwood's neck. A sixth sense he had for danger. A sense he'd had since Iraq. It had seen him through a great many situations that had left other men in a box.

He eased open the truck door and was about to step out into the night when a sharp crack of gunfire pierced the air.

Blackwood instinctively dropped down into the footwell of the truck's cabin, his heart racing with adrenaline. He had heard automatic weapons fire many times before, and it always took him back to Iraq.

He took in a deep breath and tried to reconfigure; the taste of cold, metallic fear in the back of his throat.

He raised his head above the dashboard.

A body was prone on the floor. One of the figures had his head in his hands. The other, wielding the gun, slapped him across the face. He heard the man yelling something but he couldn't make out what it was. He held his breath for what seemed like an eternity before the men headed for the truck.

They hadn't seen him, he was sure. Maybe they didn't even know he was travelling with Dag. Blackwood cursed. He should have jumped out of the cab and run for cover. He had to think fast. If they found him, he'd be as dead as Dag.

Taking a deep breath, he reached up and opened the roof hatch, squeezing himself out of the small opening. He lay down on top of the truck's cabin, pressing himself flat against the cold metal surface.

They converged on the truck. Blackwood listened. The truck shifted as one of them climbed into the cab. The others went round to the rear of the truck. They hadn't seen him. They didn't know he was there.

He held his breath and listened.

A stream of Norwegian. Indecipherable but for a few odd words he recognised: *nei* and *narkotika* and something about a green locker.

Whoever was in the cab, jumped out and joined the others at the rear. The truck shuddered as the doors slid open at the back.

Blackwood used the noise as cover to climb down to the ground, landing as silently as he could, and scooting under the truck to lie in the black shade.

The figures searched the truck and lifted something out. He followed their feet as they carried whatever it was to a nearby car and threw it in the boot.

This was the moment. His chance to escape.

He rolled out from under the truck, out into the open, and jumped to his feet to come eye to eye with a startled face.

Order *Death in Oslo* on Amazon now

UNLOCK THE CANTERBURY FILE

A FREE SHORT STORY PREQUEL TO THE JOHN BLACKWOOD THRILLER SERIES

Join the John Blackwood Shadow Network today and immediately receive The Canterbury File, an exclusive short story prequel only available to Shadow Network members.

Uncover the details of Blackwood's last mission for Clocktower, the off-the-books assassination squad that shaped him, and witness the betrayal that sets the stage for the entire John Blackwood Thriller series.

https://subscribepage.io/CanterburyFile

Acknowledgements

Very special thanks are due to Steve Bond, who provided much of the information underpinning this story, with fascinating insights into the Finnmark border and the mystery of a certain downed flight during operation Able Archer.

Author Jack Turner again provided invaluable advice on all aspects of the military, weaponry and murder.

Thanks also to everyone at Wallbank Books for their hardworking support and encouragement, but mostly to editor David Wake, who demands perfection, deserves a pint, and whose own brilliant books can be found at davidwake.com.

About the Author

Andy Conway is a novelist and screenwriter who publishes the John Blackwood thrillers, the best-selling Touchstone historical fantasy saga, and the Dartmoor Noir series. He lives in Birmingham with his wife and two ginger cats, and runs a publishing empire from his loft.

Also from Wallbank Books

Step into the gritty world of Howie Earls, the Black journalist who digs up the dirt other hacks won't touch.

Chuck Loyola's hardboiled crime series delivers classic private eye pulp noir with a modern edge. Think Raymond Chandler with a British accent and a protagonist who's got more to lose than just his press pass.

Available in Kindle, paperback and Kindle Unlimited.

Printed in Dunstable, United Kingdom

70442818R00214